John Parker Anderson, William Michael Rossetti

Life of John Keats

John Parker Anderson, William Michael Rossetti

Life of John Keats

ISBN/EAN: 9783337415815

Printed in Europe, USA, Canada, Australia, Japan

Cover: Foto ©Raphael Reischuk / pixelio.de

More available books at **www.hansebooks.com**

LIFE

OF

JOHN KEATS.

BY

WILLIAM MICHAEL ROSSETTI.

LONDON
WALTER SCOTT
24 WARWICK LANE, PATERNOSTER ROW
1887

CONTENTS.

CHAPTER VI.

CHAPTER VII.

CHAPTER VIII.

CHAPTER IX.

8 *CONTENTS.*

PAGE

NOTE.

IN all important respects I leave this brief "Life of Keats" to speak for itself. There is only one point which I feel it needful to dwell upon. In the summer of 1886 I was invited to undertake a life of Keats for the present series, and I assented. Some while afterwards it was publicly announced that a life of Keats, which had been begun by Mr. Sidney Colvin long before for a different series, would be published at an early date. I read up my materials, began in March 1887 the writing of my book, finished it on June 3rd, and handed it over to the editor. On June 10th Mr. Colvin's volume was published. I at once read it, and formed a high opinion of its merits, and I found in it some new details which could not properly be ignored by any succeeding biographer of the poet. I therefore got my MS. back, and inserted here and there such items of fresh information as were really needful for the true presentment of my subject-matter. In justice both to Mr. Colvin and to myself I drew upon his pages for only a minimum, not a maximum, of the facts which they embody; and in all matters of opinion and criticism I left my MS. exactly as it stood. The reader will thus understand that the present "Life of Keats" is, in planning, structure, execution, and estimate, entirely independent of Mr. Colvin's; but that I have ultimately had the advantage of consulting Mr. Colvin's book as one of my various sources of information—the latest and within its own lines the completest of all.

LIFE OF KEATS.

CHAPTER I

A TRUISM must do duty as my first sentence
There are long lives, and there are eventful lives :
there are also short lives, and uneventful ones. Keats's
life was both short and uneventful. To the differing
classes of lives different modes of treatment may properly be applied by the biographer. In the case of a
writer whose life was both long and eventful, I might feel
disposed to carry the whole narrative forward *pari passu*,
and to exhibit in one panorama the outward and the
inward career, the incidents and the product, the doings
and environment, and the writings, acting and re-acting
upon one another. In the instance of Keats this does
not appear to me to be the most fitting method. It may
be more appropriate to apportion his Life into two sec-
tions : and to treat firstly of his general course from the
cradle to the grave, and secondly of his performances in
literature. The two things will necessarily overlap to
some extent, but I shall keep them apart so far as may
be convenient. When we have seen what he did and
what he wrote, we shall be prepared to enter upon some
analysis of his character and personality. This will form

my third section ; and in a fourth I shall endeavour to
estimate the quality and value of his writings, in particular and in general.   Thus I address myself in the first
instance to a narrative of the outer facts of his life.

John Keats came of undistinguished parentage.   No
biographer carries his pedigree further than his maternal
grandfather, or alleges that there was any trace, however
faint or remote, of ancestral eminence.   The maternal
grandfather was a Mr. Jennings, who kept a large livery-
stable, called the Swan and Hoop, in the Pavement,
Moorfields, London, opposite the entrance to Finsbury
Circus.   The principal stableman or assistant in the business was named Thomas Keats, of Devonshire or Cornish
parentage.   He was a well-conducted, sensible, good-
looking little man, and won the favour of Jennings's
daughter, named Frances or Fanny : they married, and
this rather considerable rise in his fortunes left Keats
unassuming and manly as before.   He appears to have
been a natural gentleman.   Jennings was a prosperous
tradesman, and might have died rich (his death took
place in 1805) but for easy-going good-nature tending to
the gullible.   Mrs. Keats seems to have been in character less uniform and single-minded than her husband.
She is described as passionately fond of amusement,
prodigal, dotingly attached to her children, more especially
John, much beloved by them in return, sensible, and at
the same time saturnine in demeanour : a personable tall
woman with a large oval face.   Her pleasure-seeking
tendency probably led her into some imprudences, for
her first baby, John, was a seven months' child.

John Keats was born at the Moorfields place of business on the 31st of October 1795. This date of birth is established by the register of baptisms at St. Botolph's, Bishopsgate: the date usually assigned, the 29th of October, appears to be inaccurate, though Keats himself, and others of the family, believed in it. There were three other children of the marriage—or four if we reckon a a son who died in infancy: George, Thomas, and lastly Fanny, born in March 1803. An anecdote is told of John when in the fifth year of his age, purporting to show forth the depth of his childish affection for his mother. It is said that she then lay seriously ill; and John stood sentinel at her chamber-door, holding an old sword which he had picked up about the premises, and he remained there for hours to prevent her being disturbed. One may fear, however, that this anecdote has taken an ideal colouring through the lens of a partial biographer. The painter Benjamin Robert Haydon—who, as we shall see in the sequel, was extremely well acquainted with John Keats, and who heard the story from his brother Thomas —records it thus: "He was, when an infant, a most violent and ungovernable child. At five years of age or thereabouts he once got hold of a naked sword, and, shutting the door, swore nobody should go out. His mother wanted to do so; but he threatened her so furiously she began to cry, and was obliged to wait till somebody, through the window, saw her position, and came to her rescue." It can scarcely be supposed that there were two different occasions when the quinquennial John Keats superintended his mother and her belongings with a naked sword—once in ardent and self-oblivious affection, and once in petulant and froward excitement.

The parents would have liked to send John to Harrow school : but, this being finally deemed too expensive, he was placed in the Rev. John Clarke's school at Enfield, then in high repute, and his brothers followed him thither. The Enfield schoolhouse was a fine red-brick building of the early eighteenth century, said to have been erected by a retired West India merchant; the materials "moulded into designs decorating the front with garlands of flowers and pomegranates, together with heads of cherubim over two niches in the centre of the building." This central part of the façade was eventually purchased for the South Kensington Museum, and figures there as a screen in the structural division. The schoolroom was forty feet long; the playground was a spacious courtyard between the schoolroom and the house itself; a garden, a hundred yards in length, stretched beyond the playground, succeeded by a sweep of greensward, with a "lake" or well-sized pond : there was also a two-acre field with a couple of cows. In this commodious seat of sound learning, well cared for and well instructed so far as his school course extended, John Keats remained for some years. He came under the particular observation of the headmaster's son, Mr. Charles Cowden Clarke, not very many years his senior. He was born in 1787, fostered Keats's interest in literature, became himself an industrious writer of some standing, and died in 1877. Keats at school did not show any exceptional talent, but he was, according to Mr. Cowden Clarke's phrase, "a very orderly scholar," and got easily through his tasks. In the last eighteen

months of his schooling he took a new lease of assiduity:
he read a vast deal, and would keep to his book even
during meals. For two or three successive half-years he
obtained the first prize for voluntary work; and was to
be found early and late attending to some translation
from the Latin or the French, to which he would, when
allowed his own way, sacrifice his recreation-time. He
was particularly fond of Lemprière's "Classical Diction-
ary," Tooke's "Pantheon," and Spence's "Polymetis":
a line of reading presageful of his own afterwork in the
region of Greek mythology. Of the Grecian language,
however, he learned nothing: in Latin he proceeded as
far as the Æneid, and of his own accord translated much
of that epic in writing. Two of his favourite books were
"Robinson Crusoe" and Marmontel's "Incas of Peru."
He must also have made some acquaintance with Shakespeare, as he told a younger schoolfellow that he thought
no one durst read "Macbeth" alone in the house at two
in the morning. Not indeed that these bookish leanings
formed the whole of his personality as a schoolboy. He
was noticeable for beauty of face and expression; active
and energetic, intensely pugnacious, and even quarrel-
some. He was very apt to get into a fight with boys
much bigger than himself. Nor was his younger
brother George exempted: John would fight fiercely with
George, and this (if we may trust George's testimony)
was always owing to John's own unmanageable temper.
The two brothers were none the less greatly attached,
both at school and afterwards. The youngest brother,
Thomas (always called Tom in family records), is reported
to have been as pugilistic as John; whereas George, when

allowed his own way, was pacific, albeit resolute. The
ideal of all the three boys was a maternal uncle, a naval
officer of very stalwart presence, who had been in
Admiral Duncan's ship in the famous action off Camper-
down ; where he had distinguished himself not only by
signal gallantry, but by not getting shot, though his tall
form was a continual mark for hostile guns.

While still a schoolboy at Enfield, John Keats lost both
his parents. The father died on the 16th of April 1804, in
returning from a visit to the school : a detail which serves
to show us (for I do not find it otherwise affirmed) that
John could at the utmost have been only in the ninth
year of his age, possibly even younger, when his schooling
began.   On leaving Enfield, the father dined at Southgate,
and, going late homewards, his horse fell in the City
Road, and the rider's skull was fractured.   He was found
about one o'clock in the morning speechless, and expired
towards eight, aged thirty-six.   The mother suffered from
rheumatism, and later on from consumption ; of which
she died in February 1810.   " John," so writes Haydon,
"sat up whole nights with her in a great chair, would
suffer nobody to give her medicine or even cook her food
but himself, and read novels to her in her intervals of ease."
She had been an easily consoled widow, for, within a year
from the decease of her first husband, she married another, William Rawlings, who had probably succeeded to
the management of the business.   She soon, however,
separated from Rawlings, and lived with her mother at
Edmonton.   After her death Keats hid himself for some
days in a nook under his master's desk, passionately in-
consolable.   The four children, who inherited from their
grandparents (chiefly from their grandmother) a moderate

fortune of nearly £8,000 altogether, in which the daughter had the largest share, were then left under the guardianship of Mr. Abbey, a city merchant residing at Walthamstow. At the age of fifteen, or at some date before the close of 1810, John quitted his school.

A little stave of doggrel which Keats wrote to his sister, probably in July 1818, gives a glimpse of what he was like at the time when he and his brothers were living with their grandmother.

> "There was a naughty boy,
> And a naughty boy was he :
> He kept little fishes
> In washing-tubs three,
>   In spite
>   Of the might
>   Of the maid,
>   Nor afraid
> Of his granny good.
> He often would
> Hurly-burly
> Get up early
>   And go
> By hook or crook
> To the brook,
> And bring home
> Miller's-thumb,
> Tittlebat,
> Not over fat,
> Minnows small
> As the stall
> Of a glove,
> Not above
>   The size
>   Of a nice
> Little baby's
> Little fingers."

He was fond of "goldfinches, tomtits, minnows, mice,
ticklebacks, dace, cock-salmons, and all the whole tribe of
the bushes and the brooks."

A career in life was promptly marked out for the youth.
While still aged fifteen, he was apprenticed, with a pre-
mium of £210, to Mr. Hammond, a surgeon of some
repute at Edmonton. Mr. Cowden Clarke says that this
arrangement evidently gave Keats satisfaction: apparently
he refers rather to the convenient vicinity of Edmonton
to Enfield than to the surgical profession itself. The
indenture was to have lasted five years; but, for some
reason which is not wholly apparent, Keats left Hammond
before the close of his apprenticeship.[1] If Haydon was
rightly informed (presumably by Keats himself), the
reason was that the youth resented surgery as the antago-
nist of a possible poetic vocation, and "at last his master,
weary of his disgust, gave him up his time." He then
took to walking St. Thomas's Hospital; and, after a short

---

[1] A small point here may deserve a note. A letter from John
Keats to his brother George, under date of September 21st, 1819,
contains the following words: "Our bodies, every seven years, are
completely fresh-materialed: seven years ago it was not this hand
that clenched itself against Hammond." Another version of the
same letter (the true wording of which is matter of some dispute)
substitutes: "Mine is not the same hand I clenched at Hammond's."
Mr. Buxton Forman, who gives the former phrase as the genuine
one, thinks that "this phrase points to a serious rupture as the cause
of his quitting his apprenticeship to Hammond." My own inclination is to surmise that the accurate reading may be—"It was not
this hand that clenched itself against Hammond's"; indicating, not
any quarrel, but the friendly habitual clasp of hand against hand.
"Seven years ago" would reach back to September 1812: whereas
Keats did not part from Hammond until 1814.

stay at No. 8 Dean Street, Borough, and next in St.
Thomas's Street, he resided along with his two brothers—
who were at the time clerks in Mr. Abbey's office—in the
Poultry, Cheapside, over the passage which led to the
Queen's Arms Tavern. Two of his surgical companions
were Mr. Henry Stephens, who afterwards introduced
creosote into medical practice, and Mr. George Wilson
Mackereth. Keats attended the usual lectures, and made
careful annotations in a book still preserved. Mr.
Stephens relates that Keats was fond of scribbling rhyme
of a sort among professional notes, especially those of a
fellow-student, and he sometimes showed graver verses to
his associates. Finally, in July 1815, he passed the ex-
amination at Apothecaries' Hall with considerable credit
—more than his familiars had counted upon; and in
March 1816 he was appointed a dresser at Guy's under
Mr. Lucas. Cowden Clarke once inquired how far
Keats liked his studies at the hospital. The youth replied that he did not relish anatomy: "The other day,
for instance, during the lecture, there came a sunbeam
into the room, and with it a whole troop of creatures
floating in the ray, and I was off with them to Oberon
and fairyland."

Readers of Keats's poetry will have no difficulty in
believing that, ever since his first introduction into a
professional life, surgery and literature had claimed a
divided allegiance from him. When at Edmonton
with Mr. Hammond, he kept up his connection with
the Clarke family, especially with Charles Cowden
Clarke. He was perpetually borrowing books; and at
last, about the beginning of 1812, he asked for Spenser's

"Faery Queen," rather to the surprise of the family, who had no idea that that particular book could be at all in his line. The effect, however, was very noticeable. Keats walked to Enfield at least once a week, for the purpose of talking over Spenser with Cowden Clarke. "He ramped through the scenes of the romance," said Clarke, "like a young horse turned into a spring meadow." A fine touch of description or of imagery, or energetic epithets such as "the sea-shouldering whale," would light up his face with ecstasy. His leisure had already been given to reading and translation, including the completion of his rendering of the Æneid. A literary craving was now at fever-heat, and he took to writing verses as well as reading them. Soon surgery and letters were to conflict no longer—the latter obtaining, contrary to the liking of Mr. Abbey, the absolute and permanent mastery. Keats indeed always denied that he abandoned surgery for the express purpose of taking to poetry : he alleged that his motive had been the dread of doing some mischief in his surgical operations. His last operation consisted in opening a temporal artery ; he was entirely successful in it, but the success appeared to himself like a miracle, the recurrence of which was not to be reckoned on.

While surgery was waning with Keats, and finally dying out—an upshot for which the exact date is not assigned, nor perhaps assignable—he was making, at first through his intimacy with Cowden Clarke, some good literary acquaintances. The brothers John and Leigh Hunt were the centre of the circle to which Keats was thus admitted. John was the publisher, and Leigh the

editor, of *The Examiner*. They had both been lately
fined, and imprisoned for two years, for a libel on the
Prince Regent, George IV.; it was perhaps legally a
libel, and was certainly a castigation laid on with no
indulgent hand. Leigh Hunt (born in 1784, and therefore Keats's senior by some eleven years) is known to us
all as a fresh and airy essayist, a fresh and airy poet, a
liberal thinker in the morals both of society and of
politics (hardly a politician in the stricter sense of the
term), a charming companion, a too-constant cracker of
genial jocosities and of puns. He understood good
literature both instinctively and critically; but was too
full of tricksy mannerisms, and of petted byways in thought
and style, to be an altogether safe associate for a youthful
literary aspirant, whether as model or as Mentor. Leigh
Hunt first saw Keats in the spring of 1816, not at his
residence in Hampstead as has generally been supposed,
but at No. 8 York Buildings, New Road.[1] The earliest
meeting of Keats with Haydon was in November 1816,
at Hunt's house; Haydon born in 1786, the zealous and
impatient champion of high art, wide-minded and combative, too much absorbed in his love for art to be without a considerable measure of self-seeking for art's
apostle, himself. He painted into his large picture of
Christ's Entry into Jerusalem the head of Keats, along
with those of Wordsworth and others. Another acquaintance was Mr. Charles Ollier, the publisher, who wrote
verse and prose of his own. The Ollier firm in the early
spring of 1817 became the publishers of Keats's first

---

[1] This is Hunt's own express statement. It has been disputed,
but I am not prepared to reject it.

volume of poems, of which more anon. Still earlier
than the Hunts, Haydon, and Ollier, Keats had known
John Hamilton Reynolds, his junior by a year, a poetical
writer of some mark, now too nearly forgotten, author of
"The Garden of Florence," "The Fancy," and the prose
tale, "Miserrimus"; he was the son of the writing-master
at Christ Hospital, and Keats became intimate with the
whole family, though not invariably well pleased with
them all. One of the sisters married Thomas Hood.
Through Reynolds Keats made acquaintance with Mr.
Benjamin Bailey, born towards 1794, then a student at
Oxford reading for the Church, afterwards Archdeacon
of Colombo in Ceylon. Charles Wentworth Dilke, born
in 1789, the critic, and eventually editor of *The Athenæum*,
was another intimate; and in course of time Keats knew
Charles Wells, seven years younger than himself, the
author of the dramatic poem "Joseph and his Brethren,"
and of the prose "Stories after Nature." Other friends
will receive mention as we progress. I have for the
present said enough to indicate what was the particular
niche in the mansion of English literary life in which
Keats found himself housed at the opening of his career.

CHAPTER II.

WE have now reached the year 1817 and the month of May, when Keats was in the twenty-second year of his age. He then wrote that he had "forgotten all surgery," and was beginning at Margate his romantic epic of "Endymion," reading and writing about eight hours a day. Keats had previously been at Carisbrooke in the Isle of Wight, but had run away from there, finding that the locality, while it charmed, also depressed him. He had left London for the island, apparently with the view of having greater leisure for study and composition. His brother Tom was with him at Carisbrooke and at Margate. He was already provided with a firm of publishers, Messrs. Taylor and Hessey, willing to undertake the risk of "Endymion," and they advanced him a sum sufficient for continuing at work on it with comfort. In September he went with Mr. Benjamin Bailey to Oxford : they made an excursion to Stratford-on-Avon, and Keats was back at Hampstead by the end of the month. It would appear that in Oxford Keats, in the heat of youthful blood, committed an indiscretion of which we do not know the details, nor need we give them if we knew them ; for on the 8th of October he wrote to Bailey in

these terms : "The little mercury I have taken has cor
rected the poison and improved my health,[1] though I
feel, from my employment, that I shall never again be
secure in robustness." The residence of Keats and his
brother Tom in Hampstead, a first-floor lodging, was in
Well Walk, No. 1, next to the Wells Tavern, which was
then called the Green Man. The reader who has a head
for localities should bear this point well in mind, should
carefully discriminate the house in Well Walk from
another house, Wentworth Place, afterwards tenanted by
Keats and others at Hampstead, and, every time that the
question occurs to his thought, should pass a mental vote
of thanks to Mr. Buxton Forman for the great pains
which he took to settle the point, and the lucid and
pleasant account which he has given of it. Keats was at
Leatherhead in November ; finished the first draft of
" Endymion " at Burford Bridge, near Dorking, on the

---

[1] Biographers have been reticent on this subject. Keats's statement however speaks for itself, and a high medical authority, Dr.
Richardson, writing in *The Asclepiad* for April 1884, and reviewing
the whole subject of the poet's constitutional and other ailments,
says that Keats in Oxford "runs loose, and pays a forfeit for his
indiscretion which ever afterwards physically and morally embarrasses
him." He pronounces that Keats's early death was "expedited,
perhaps excited, by his own imprudence," but was substantially due
to hereditary disease. His mother, as we have already seen, had
died of the malady which killed the poet, consumption. It is not
clear to me what Keats meant by saying that "from his *employment* "
his health would be insecure. One might suppose that he was
thinking of the long and haphazard working hours of a young
surgeon or medical man ; in which case, this seems to be the latest
instance in which he spoke of himself as still belonging to that
profession.

28th of that month, and returned to Hampstead for the winter. Two anecdotes which have often been repeated belong apparently to about this date. One of them purports that Keats gave a sound drubbing in Hampstead to a butcher, or a butcher's boy, who was ill-treating a small boy, or else a cat. Hunt simply says that the butcher "had been insolent,"—by implication, to Keats himself. The "butcher's boy" has obtained traditional currency; but, according to George Keats, the offender was "a scoundrel in livery," the locality "a blind alley at Hampstead." Clarke says that the stand-up fight lasted nearly an hour. Keats was an undersized man, in fact he was not far removed from the dwarfish, being barely more than five feet high, and this small feat of stubborn gallantry deserves to be appraised and praised accordingly. The other anecdote is that Coleridge met Keats along with Leigh Hunt in a lane near Highgate, "a loose, slack, not well-dressed youth," and after shaking hands with Keats, he said aside to Hunt, "There is death in that hand." Nothing is extant to show that at so early a date as this, or even for some considerable while after, any of Keats's immediate friends shared the ominous prevision of Coleridge.

In March 1818 Keats joined his brothers at Teignmouth in Devonshire, and in April "Endymion" was published. In June he set off on a pedestrian tour of some extent with a friend whose name will frequently recur from this point forwards, Charles Armitage Brown. One is generally inclined to get some idea of what a man was like; if one knows what he was *un*like much the same purpose is served. In April 1819 Keats wrote

some bantering verses about Brown, which are understood to go mainly by contraries: we therefore infer
Brown to have presented a physical and moral aspect
the reverse of the following—

" He is to meet a melancholy carle,
      Thin in the waist, with bushy head of hair,
  As hath the seeded thistle when a parle
      It holds with Zephyr ere it sendeth fair
      Its light balloons into the summer air.
  Thereto his beard had not begun to bloom ;
      No brush had touched his chin, or razor sheer ;
  No care had touched his cheek with mortal doom,
But new he was and bright as scarf from Persian loom.

" Ne carèd he for wine or half-and-half,
      Ne carèd he for fish or flesh or fowl,
  And sauces held he worthless as the chaff ;
      He 'sdained the swine-head at the wassail bowl.
  Ne with lewd ribalds sat he cheek by jowl,
      Ne with sly lemans in the scorner's chair ;
  But after water-brooks this pilgrim's soul
  Panted, and all his food was woodland air,
Though he would oft-times feast on gillyflowers rare.

" The slang of cities in no wise he knew ;
      ' Tipping the wink ' to him was heathen Greek.
  He sipped no olden Tom or ruin blue,
      Or Nantz or cherry-brandy, drank full meek
      By many a damsel brave and rouge of cheek.
  Nor did he know each aged watchman's beat ;
      Nor in obscurèd purlieus would he seek
  For curlèd Jewesses with ankles neat,
Who, as they walk abroad, make tinkling with their feet."

Mr. Brown, son of a London stockbroker from Scotland,
was a man several years older than Keats, born in 1786.

He was a Russia merchant retired from business, of much culture and instinctive sympathy with genius, and he enjoyed assisting the efforts of young men of promise. He had produced the libretto of an opera, " Narensky," and he eventually published a book on the Sonnets of Shakespeare. From the date we have now reached, the summer of 1818, which was more than a year following their first introduction, Brown may be regarded as the most intimate of all Keats's friends, Dilke coming next to him.

The pedestrian tour with Brown was the sequel of a family leave-taking at Liverpool. George Keats, finding in himself no vocation for trade, with its smug compliances and sleek assiduities (and John agreed with him in these views), had determined to emigrate to America, and rough it in a new settlement for a living, perhaps for fortune ; and, as a preliminary step, he had married Miss Georgiana Augusta Wylie, a girl of sixteen, daughter of a deceased naval officer. The sonnet " Nymph of the downward smile " &c. was addressed to her. John Keats and Brown, therefore, accompanied George and his bride to Liverpool, and saw them off. They then started as pedestrians into the Lake country, the land of Burns, Belfast, and the Western Highlands. Before starting on the trip Keats had often been in such a state of health as to make it prudent that he should not hazard exposure to night air ; but in his excursion he seems to have acted like a man of sound and rather hardy physique, walking from day to day about twenty miles, and sometimes more, and his various records of the trip have nothing of a morbid or invaliding tone. This was not,

however, to last long; the Isle of Mull proved too much
for him. On the 23rd of July, writing to his brother
Tom, he describes the expedition thus: "The road
through the island, or rather track, is the most dreary
you can think of; between dreary mountains, over bog
and rock and river, with our breeches tucked up and our
stockings in hand. . . . We had a most wretched walk of
thirty-seven miles across the island of Mull, and then we
crossed to Iona." In another letter he says: "Walked
up to my knees in bog; got a sore throat; gone to see
Icolmkill and Staffa." From this time forward the mention of the sore throat occurs again and again; sometimes
it is subsiding, or as good as gone; at other times it has
returned, and causes more or less inconvenience. Brown
wrote of it as "a violent cold and ulcerated throat." The
latest reference to it comes in December 1819, only two
months preceding the final and alarming break-down in
the young poet's health. In Scotland, at any rate, amid
the exposure and exertion of the walking tour, the sore
throat was not to be staved off; so, having got as far as
Inverness, Keats, under medical advice, reluctantly cut
his journey short, parted from Brown, and went on board
the smack from Cromarty. A nine days' passage brought
him to London Bridge, and on the 18th of August he
presented himself to the rather dismayed eyes of Mrs.
Dilke. "John Keats," she wrote, "arrived here last
night, as brown and as shabby as you can imagine:
scarcely any shoes left, his jacket all torn at the back, a
fur cap, a great plaid, and his knapsack. I cannot tell
what he looked like." More ought to be said here of
the details of Keats's Scottish and Irish trip; but such

details, not being of essential importance as incidents in his life, could only be given satisfactorily in the form of copious extracts from his letters, and for these—readable and picturesque as they are—I have not adequate space. He preferred, on the whole, the Scotch people to the little which he saw of the Irish. Just as Keats was leaving Scotland, because of his own ailments, he had been summoned away thence on account of the more visibly grave malady of his brother Tom, who was in an advanced stage of consumption; but it appears that the letter did not reach his hands at the time.

The next three months were passed by Keats along with Tom at their Hampstead lodgings. Anxiety and affection—warm affection, deep anxiety—were of no avail. Tom died at the beginning of December, aged just twenty, and was buried on the 7th of that month. The words in "King Lear," "Poor Tom," remain underlined by the surviving brother.

John Keats was now solitary in the world. Tom was dead, George and his bride in America, Fanny, his girlish sister, a permanent inmate of the household of Mr. and Mrs. Abbey at Walthamstow. In December he quitted his lodgings at Hampstead, and set up house along with Mr. Brown in what was then called Wentworth Place, Hampstead, now Lawn Bank; Brown being rightly the tenant, and Keats a paying resident with Brown. Wentworth Place consisted of only two houses. One of them was thus inhabited by Brown and Keats, the other by the Dilkes. In the first of these houses, when Brown and Keats were away, and afterwards in the second, there was also a well-to-do family of the name of Brawne,—a

mother, with a son and two daughters. Lawn Bank is
the penultimate house on the right of John Street, next
to Wentworth House : Dr. Sharpey passed some of his
later years in it. This is, beyond all others, the dwelling
which remains permanently linked with the memory of
Keats.

While Tom was still lingering out the days of his brief
life, Keats made the acquaintance of two young ladies.
He has left us a description of both of them. His portraiture of the first, Miss Jane Cox, is written in a tone
which might seem the preliminary to a *grande passion ;*
but this did not prove so ; she rapidly passed out of his
existence and out of his memory. His portraiture of the
second, Miss Fanny Brawne, does not suggest anything
beyond a tepid liking which might perhaps merge into
a definite antipathy ; this also was delusive, for he was
from the first smitten with Miss Brawne, and soon profoundly in love with her—I might say desperately in
love, for indeed desperation, which became despair, was
the main ingredient in his passion, in all but its earliest
stages. I shall here extract these two passages, for both
of them are of exceptional importance for our biography—
one as acquainting us with Keats's general range of feeling
in relation to women, and the other as introducing the
most serious and absorbing sentiment of the last two
years of his life. On October 29, 1818, he wrote as
follows to his brother George and his wife in America :—

"The Misses Reynolds are very kind to me. . . . On
my return, the first day I called [this was probably towards the 20th of September], they were in a sort of

taking or bustle about a cousin of theirs, Miss Cox, who, having fallen out with her grandpapa in a serious manner, was invited by Mrs. Reynolds to take asylum in her house. She is an East Indian, and ought to be her grandfather's heir. . . . From what I hear she is not without faults of a real kind; but she has others which are more apt to make women of inferior claims hate her. She is not a Cleopatra, but is at least a Charmian; she has a rich Eastern look; she has fine eyes and fine manners. When she comes into the room she makes the same impression as the beauty of a leopardess. She is too fine and too conscious of herself to repulse any man who may address her; from habit she thinks that nothing particular. I always find myself more at ease with such a woman; the picture before me always gives me a life and animation which I cannot possibly feel with anything inferior. I am at such times too much occupied in admiring to be awkward or in a tremble; I forget myself entirely, because I live in her. You will by this time think I am in love with her; so, before I go any further, I will tell you I am not. She kept me awake one night, as a tune of Mozart's might do. I speak of the thing as a pastime and an amusement, than which I can feel none deeper than a conversation with an imperial woman, the very yes and no of whose lips [1] is to me a banquet. I don't cry to take the moon home with me in my pocket, nor do I fret to leave her behind me. I like her, and her like, because one has no *sensations;* what we both are is taken for granted. You will suppose I have by

[1] Hitherto printed "life"; it seems to me clear that "lips" is the right word.

this time had much talk with her. No such thing; there are the Misses Reynolds on the look out. They think I don't admire her because I don't stare at her; they call her a flirt to me—what a want of knowledge! She walks across a room in such a manner that a man is drawn to her with a magnetic power; this they call flirting! They do not know things; they do not know what a woman is. I believe, though, she has faults, the same as Charmian and Cleopatra might have had. Yet she is a fine thing, speaking in a worldly way; for there are two distinct tempers of mind in which we judge of things :—the worldly, theatrical, and pantomimical; and the unearthly, spiritual, and ethereal. In the former, Bonaparte, Lord Byron, and this Charmian, hold the first place in our mind; in the latter, John Howard, Bishop Hooker rocking his child's cradle, and you, my dear sister, are the conquering feelings. As a man of the world, I love the rich talk of a Charmian; as an eternal being, I love the thought of you. I should like her to ruin me, and I should like you to save me."

So much for Miss Cox, the Charmian whom Keats was not in love with. This is not absolutely the sole mention of her in his letters, but it is the only one of importance. We now turn to Miss Brawne, the young lady with whom he had fallen very much in love at a date even preceding that to which the present description must belong. The description comes from a letter to George and Georgiana Keats, written probably towards the middle of December 1818. It is true that the name Brawne does not appear in the printed version of the letter, but the " very positive conviction " expressed by Mr. Forman that that name really does stand in the MS., a conviction "shared by members of her family," may safely be adopted by all my readers. I therefore insert the name where a blank had heretofore appeared in print.

" Perhaps, as you are fond of giving me sketches of characters, you may like a little picnic of scandal, even across the Atlantic. Shall I give you Miss Brawne ? She is about my height, with a fine style of countenance of the lengthened sort. She wants sentiment in every feature. She manages to make her hair look well ; her nostrils are very fine, though a little painful ; her mouth is bad, and good ; her profile is better than her full face, which indeed is not 'full,' but pale and thin, without showing any bone ; her shape is very graceful, and so are her movements ; her arms are good, her hands bad-ish, her feet tolerable. She is not seventeen [Keats, if he really wrote ' not seventeen,' was wrong here ; ' not nineteen ' would have been correct, as she was born on August 9, 1800.] But she is ignorant, monstrous in her behaviour, flying out in all directions ; calling people such names that I was forced lately to make use of the term ' minx.' This is, I think, from no innate vice, but from a penchant she has for acting stylishly. I am, however, tired of such style, and shall decline any more of it. She had a friend to visit her lately. You have known plenty such. She plays the music, but without one sensation but the feel of the ivory at her fingers. She is a downright Miss, without one set-off. We hated her ["We" would apparently be Keats, Brown, and the

Dilkes], and smoked her, and baited her, and I think drove her away. Miss Brawne thinks her a paragon of fashion, and says she is the only woman in the world she would change persons with. What a stupe! She is as superior as a rose to a dandelion."

At the time when Keats wrote these words he had known Miss Brawne for a couple of months, more or less, having first seen her in October or November at the house of the Dilkes. It might seem that he was about this time in a state of feeling propense to love. *Some* woman was required to fill the void in his heart. The woman might have been Miss Cox, whom he met in September. As the event turned out, it was not she, but it *was* Miss Brawne, whom he met in October or November. Fanny Brawne was the elder daughter of a gentleman of independent means, who died while she was still a child; he left another daughter and a son with their mother; and the whole family, as already mentioned, lived at times in the same house which the Dilkes occupied in Wentworth-place, Hampstead, and at other times in the adjoining house, while not tenanted by Brown and Keats. Miss Brawne (I quote here from Mr. Forman) " had much natural pride and buoyancy, and was quite capable of affecting higher spirits and less concern than she really felt. But, as to the genuineness of her attachment to Keats, some of those who knew her personally have no doubt whatever."[1] If so—or indeed

---

[1] In Medwin's " Life of Shelley," vol. ii. pp. 89 to 92, are some interesting remarks upon Keats's character and demeanour, written in a warm and sympathetic tone. Some of them were certainly

whether so or not—it is a pity that she was wont, after
Keats's death, to speak of him (as has been averred) as
"that foolish young poet who was in love with me." That
Keats was a poet and a young poet is abundantly true;
but that he was a foolish one had even before his death,
and especially very soon after it, been found out to be a
gross delusion by a large number of people, and might
just as well have been found out by his betrothed bride
in addition. I know of only one portrait of Miss Brawne;
it is a silhouette by Edouart, engraved in two of Mr.
Forman's publications. A silhouette is one of the least
indicative forms of portraiture for enabling one to judge
whether the sitter was handsome or not. This likeness
shows a very profuse mass of hair, a tall, rather sloping,
forehead, a long and prominent aquiline nose, a mouth
and chin of the *petite* kind, a very well-developed throat,
and a figure somewhat small in proportion to the head.
The face is not of the sort which I should suppose to
have ever been beautiful in an artist's eyes, or in a poet's
either; and indeed Keats's description of Miss Brawne,
which I have just cited, is qualified, chilly, and critical,
with regard to beauty. Nevertheless, his love-letters to
Miss Brawne, most of which have been preserved and
published, speak of her beauty very emphatically. "The
very first week I knew you I wrote myself your vassal;"
"I cannot conceive any beginning of such love as I have
for you, but beauty;" "all I can bring you is a swooning

penned by Miss Brawne (Mrs. Lindon), and possibly all of them.
Mr. Colvin (p. 233 of his book) has called special attention to these
remarks: I forbear from quoting them. A leading point is to
vindicate Keats from the imputation of "violence of temper."

admiration of your beauty." It seems probable that
Keats was the declared lover of Miss Brawne in April
1819 at the latest—more probably in February; and
when his first published letter to her was written, July
1819, he and she must certainly have been already
engaged, or all but engaged, to marry. This was contrary to Mrs. Brawne's liking. They appear to have con-
templated—anything but willingly on the poet's part—a
tolerably long engagement; for he was a young man of
twenty-three, with stinted means, no regular profession,
and no occupation save that of producing verse derided
in the high places of criticism. He spoke indeed of
re-studying in Edinburgh for the medical profession:
this was a vague notion, with which no practical beginning was made. An early marriage, followed by a year
or so of pleasuring and of intellectual advancement in
some such place as Rome or Zurich, was what Keats
really longed for.

We must now go back a little—to December 1818.
Haydon was then still engaged upon his picture of
Christ's Entry into Jerusalem, and found his progress
impeded by want of funds, and by a bad attack, from
which he frequently suffered, of weakness of eyesight.
On the 22nd of the month, Keats, with conspicuous
generosity—and although he had already lent nearly
£200 to various friends—tendered him any money-aid
which might be in his power; asking merely that his
friend would claim the fulfilment of his promise only in
the last resort. On January 7, 1819, Haydon definitely
accepted his offer; and Keats wrote back, hoping to
comply, and refusing to take any interest. His own

money affairs were, however, at this time almost at a dead-lock, controlled by lawyers and by his ex-guardian Mr. Abbey; and the amount which he had expected to command as coming to him after his brother Tom's death was not available. He had to explain as much in April 1819 to Haydon, who wrote with some urgency. Eventually he did make a small loan to the painter—£30; but very shortly afterwards (June 17th) was compelled to ask for a reimbursement—"do borrow or beg some-how what you can for me." There was a chancery-suit of old standing, begun soon after the death of Mr. Jennings in 1805, and it continued to obstruct Keats in his money affairs. The precise facts of these were also but ill-known to the poet, who had potentially at his disposal certain funds which remained *perdu* and unused until two years after his death. On September 20, 1819, he wrote to his brother George in America that Haydon had been unable to make the repayment; and he added, "He did not seem to care much about it, and let me go without my money with almost nonchalance, when he ought to have sold his drawings to supply me. I shall perhaps still be acquainted with him, but, for friendship, that is at an end." And in fact the hitherto very ardent cordiality between the poet and the painter does seem to have been materially damped after this date; Keats being somewhat reserved towards Haydon, and Haydon finding more to censure than to extol in the conduct of Keats. We can feel with both of them; and, while we pronounce Keats blameless and even praiseworthy throughout, may infer Haydon to have been not greatly blameable.

Towards the end of June 1819 Keats went to Shank-

lin ; his first companion there being an invalid but witty
and cheerful friend, James Rice, a solicitor, and his
second, Brown, who co-operated at this time with the
poet in producing the drama " Otho the Great." Next,
the two friends went to Winchester, "chiefly," wrote
Keats to his sister Fanny, "for the purpose of being near
a tolerable library, which after all is not to be found in
this place. However, we like it very much ; it is the
pleasantest town I ever was in, and has the most recom-
mendations of any." One of his letters from here
(September 21) speaks of his being now almost as well
acquainted with Italian as with French, and he adds, " I
shall set myself to get complete in Latin, and there my
learning must stop. I do not think of venturing upon
Greek." It is stated that he learned Italian with un-
common quickness.

Early in the winter which closed 1819 George Keats
came over for a short while from America, his main
object being to receive his share of the money accruing
from the decease of his brother Tom, to the cost of
whose illness he had largely contributed. He had been
in Cincinnati, and had engaged in business, but as yet
without any success. In some lines which John Keats
addressed to Miss Brawne in October there is an energetic
and no doubt consciously overloaded denunciation of
" that most hateful land, dungeoner of my friends, that
monstrous region," &c., &c. John, it appears, concealed from George, during his English visit, the fact
that he himself was then much embarrassed in money-
matters, and almost wholly dependent upon his friends
for a subsistence meanwhile ; and George left England

again without doing anything for his brother's relief or convenience. He took with him £700, some substantial part of which appears to have been the property of John, absolutely or contingently; and he undertook to remit shortly to his brother £200, to be raised by the sale of a boat which he owned in America; but months passed, and the £200 never came, no purchaser for the boat being procurable. Out of the £1,100 which Tom Keats had left, George received £440, John hardly more than £200, George thus repaying himself some money which had been previously advanced for John's professional education. For all this he has been very severely censured, Mr. Brown being among his sternest and most persistent assailants. It must seemingly have been to George Keats, and yet not to him exclusively, that Colonel Finch referred in the letter which reached Shelley's eyes, saying that John had been " infamously treated by the very persons whom his generosity had rescued from want and woe ; " and Shelley re-enforced this accusation in his preface to " Adonais "—" hooted from the stage of life, no less by those on whom he had wasted the promise of his genius than those on whom he had lavished his fortune and his care." From these painful charges George Keats eventually vindicated himself with warmth of feeling, and with so much solidity of demonstration as availed to convince Mr. Dilke, and also Mr. Abbey. Who were the other offenders glanced at by Colonel Finch, as also in one of Severn's letters, I have no distinct idea.

CHAPTER III.

FROM this point forwards nothing but misery remains to be recorded of John Keats. The narrative becomes depressing to write and depressing to read. The sensation is like that of being confined in a dark vault at noonday. One knows, indeed, that the sun of the poet's genius is blazing outside, and that, on emerging from the vault, we shall be restored to light and warmth; but the atmosphere within is not the less dark and laden, nor the shades the less murky. In tedious wretchedness, racked and dogged with the pang of body and soul, exasperated and protesting, raging now, and now ground down into patience and acceptance, Keats gropes through the valley of the shadow of death.

Before detailing the facts, we must glance for a minute at the position. Keats had a passionate ambition and a passionate love—the ambition to be a poet, the love of Fanny Brawne. At the beginning of 1820, he was conscious of his authentic vocation as a poet, and conscious also that this vocation, though recognized in a small and to some extent an influential circle, was publicly denied and ridiculed; his portion was the hiss

of the viper and the gander, the hooting of the impostor
and the owl.   His forthcoming volume was certain to
share the same fate; he knew its claims would be perversely resisted and cruelly repudiated.   If he could
make no serious impression as a poet, not only was his
leading ambition thwarted, but he would also be impeded
in getting any other and more paying literary work to
do—regular profession or employment he had none.
He was at best a poor man, and, for the while, almost
bereft of any command of funds.   So long as this state of
things, or anything like it, continued, he would be unable
to marry the woman of his heart.   While sickness kept
him a prisoner, he was torn by ideas of her volatility and
fickleness.   Disease was sapping his vitals, pain wrung
him, Death beckoned him with finger more and more
imperative.   Poetic fame became the vision of Tantalus,
and love the clasp of Ixion.

Such was the life, or such the incipient death, of
Keats, in the last twelvemonth of his brief existence.

For half a year prior to February 1820 he had been
unrestful and cheerless.   "Either that gloom overspread
me," so he wrote to James Rice, "or I was suffering under
some passionate feeling, or, if I turned to versify, that ex-
acerbated the poison of either sensation."   He began taking
laudanum at times, but was induced by Brown, towards
the end of 1819, to promise to give up this insidious
practice.   Then came the crash: it was at Hampstead, on
the night of the 3rd of February.

"One night, about eleven o'clock," I quote the words
of Lord Houghton, which have become classical, "Keats

returned home[1] in a state of strange physical excitement;
it might have appeared, to those who did not know him,
one of fierce intoxication.   He told his friend [Brown]
he had been outside the stage-coach, had received a
severe chill, was a little fevered; but added: 'I don't
feel it now.'   He was easily persuaded to go to bed;
and, as he leapt into the cold sheets, before his head was
on the pillow, he slightly coughed, and said: 'That is
blood from my mouth.   Bring me the candle: let me
see this blood.'   He gazed steadfastly some moments at
the ruddy stain, and then, looking in his friend's face
with an expression of sudden calmness never to be
forgotten, said: 'I know the colour of that blood—it is
arterial blood.   I cannot be deceived in that colour.
That drop is my death-warrant; I must die.'"

A surgeon arrived shortly, bled Keats, and pronounced
the rupture to be unimportant, but the patient was not
satisfied.   He wrote to Miss Brawne some few days
afterwards, "So violent a rush of blood came to my
lungs that I felt nearly suffocated."   By the 6th of the
month, however, he was already better, and he then said

[1] This passage is taken from Lord Houghton's "Life, &c., of
Keats," first published in 1848, and by "home" he certainly means
Wentworth Place, Hampstead.   Yet in his Aldine Edition of
Keats, his lordship says that the poet "was at that time, very much
against Mr. Brown's desire and advice, living alone in London."
This latter statement may possibly be correct—I question it.   The
passage, as written by Lord Houghton, is condensed from the
narrative of Brown.   The latter is given verbatim in Mr. Colvin's
"Keats," and is, of course, the more important and interesting
of the two.   I abstain from quoting it, solely out of regard to
Mr. Colvin's rights of priority.

in a letter to his sister: "From imprudently leaving off
my great-coat in the thaw, I caught cold, which flew to
my lungs." Later on he suffered from palpitation of the
heart; but was so far recovered by the 25th of March
as to be able to go to town to the exhibition of Haydon's
picture, Christ's Entry into Jerusalem, and early in April
he could take a walk of five miles. In March he had
written that he was then picking up flesh, and, if he
could avoid inflammation for six weeks, might yet do
well; in April his doctor assured him that his only
malady was nervous irritability and general weakness,
caused by anxiety and by the excitement of poetry. At
an untoward time for his health, about the first week in
May, Keats was obliged to quit his residence in Hampstead; as Brown was then leaving for Scotland, and,
according to his wont, let the house. Keats accordingly
went to live in Wesleyan Place, Kentish Town. A letter
which he wrote just before his departure speaks of his
uncertain outlook; he might be off to South America,
or, more likely, embarking as surgeon on a vessel trading
to the East Indies. This latter idea had been in his mind
for about a year past, off and on. What he could have con-
templated doing in South America is by no means
apparent. On the 7th of May Keats parted at Gravesend
from Brown, and they never met again. The hand with
which he grasped Brown's, and which he had of old
"clenched against Hammond's," was now, according to
his own words, "that of a man of fifty."

. Things had thus gone on pretty well with Keats's
health since he first began to rally from the blood-
spitting attack of the 3rd of February; but this was not

to continue. On the 22nd of June he again broke a
blood-vessel, and vomited blood morning and evening.
Leigh Hunt thought it high time to intervene, and
removed the patient to his house, No. 13 Mortimer
Terrace, Kentish Town. By the 7th of July—just about
the time when Keats's last volume was published, the
one containing "Lamia," "Hyperion," and all his best
works—the physician had told him that he must not
remain in England, but go to Italy. On the 12th, Mrs.
Gisborne, the friend of Godwin and of Shelley, saw him
at Hunt's house, looking emaciated, and "under sentence of death from Dr. Lamb." Three days afterwards
he wrote to Haydon "I am afraid I shall pop off just
when my mind is able to run alone." The stay at Leigh
Hunt's house came to an end in a way which speaks
volumes for the shattered nerves, and consequent morbid
susceptibility, of Keats. On the 10th of August a note
for. him written by Miss Brawne, which "contained not
a word of the least consequence," arrived at the house.
Keats was then resting in his own room, and Mrs. Hunt,
who was occupied, desired a female servant to give it to
him. The servant quitted the household on the following day ; and, in leaving, she handed the letter to Thornton
Hunt, then a mere child, asking him to reconsign it to
his mother. When Thornton did this on the 12th, the
letter was open ; opened (one assumes) either by the
servant through idle curiosity, or by Thornton through
simple childishness. " Poor Keats was affected by this
inconceivable circumstance beyond what can be imagined.
He wept for several hours, and resolved, notwithstanding
Hunt's entreaties, to leave the house. He went to

Hampstead that same evening." In Hampstead he had at least the solace of being received into the dwelling occupied by the Brawne family, being the same dwelling (next door to that of Brown and Keats) which had been recently tenanted by the Dilkes; yet the excitement or feeling, consequent on the continual presence of Miss Brawne, was perhaps harmful to him. Here he remained until the time for journeying to Italy arrived. He was still, it seems, left in some uncertainty as to the precise nature and gravity of his disease, for on the 14th of August he wrote to his sister: "'Tis not yet consumption, I believe; but it would be, were I to remain in this climate all the winter." Anyhow, his expectations of recovery, or of marked benefit from the Italian sojourn, were but faint.

Something may here be said of the love-letters of Keats to Fanny Brawne. They begin (as already stated) on the 1st of July 1819, and end at some date between his leaving Hampstead, early in May 1820, and quitting Hunt's house in August. We may assume the 10th July 1820, or thereabouts, as the date of the last letter. I cannot say that the character of Keats gains to my eyes from the perusal of this correspondence. Love-letters are not expected to be models of self-regulation and "the philosophic mind"; they would be bad love-letters, or letters of a bad specimen of a lover, if they were so. Still, one wants a man to show himself, *quâ* lover, at his highest in letters of this stamp; one wants to find in them his noblest self, his steadiest as his most ardent aspirations, in one direction. Keats seems to me, throughout his love-letters, unbalanced, wayward, and profuse; he ex-

hibits great fervour of temperament, and abundant
caressingness, without the inner depth of tenderness
and regard. He lives in his mistress, for himself. As
the letters pass further and further into the harsh black
shadows of disease, he abandons all self-restraint, and
lashes out right and left; he wills that his friends should
have been disloyal to him, as the motive for his being
disloyal to them. To make allowance for all this is
possible, and even necessary; but to treat it as not need-
ing that any allowance should be made would seem to
me futile. In the earlier letters of the series we have to
note a few points of biographic interest. He says that
he believes Miss Brawne liked him for himself, not for
his writings, and he loves her the more for it; that, on
first falling in love with her, he had written to declare
himself, but he burned the letter, fancying that she had
shown some dislike to him; that he had all his life been
indifferent to money matters, but must be chary of the
resources of his friends; that he was afraid of her "being
a little inclined to the Cressid"—one of the various
passages which show that he chafed at her girlish liking
for general society and diversions. On the 10th of
October 1819 he had had "a thousand kisses" from
her, and was resolved not to dispense with the thousand
and first. Early in June 1820 he speaks of her having
"been in the habit of flirting with Brown," who "did not
know he was doing me to death by inches."—It may be
well to give three of the letters as specimens :—

(I.)

"25 COLLEGE STREET.

"[Postmark] 13 *October* 1819.

"MY DEAREST GIRL,—This moment I have set my-self to copy some verses out fair. I cannot proceed with any degree of content. I must write you a line or two, and see if that will assist in dismissing you from my mind for ever so short a time. Upon my soul I can think of nothing else. The time is past when I had power to advise and warn you against the unpromising morning of my life. My love has made me selfish. I cannot exist without you; I am forgetful of everything but seeing you again; my life seems to stop there—I see no further. You have absorbed me; I have a sensation at the present moment as though I was dissolving. I should be exquisitely miserable without the hope of soon seeing you; I should be afraid to separate myself far from you. My sweet Fanny, will your heart never change? My love, will it? I have no limit now to my love.

"Your note came in just here. I cannot be 'happier' away from you; 'tis richer than an argosy of pearls. Do not threat me, even in jest. I have been astonished that men could die martyrs for religion—I have shuddered at it. I shudder no more; I could be martyred for *my* religion. Love is my religion—I could die for that; I could die for you. My creed is love, and you are its only tenet. You have ravished me away by a power I cannot resist; and yet I could resist till I saw you; and even since I have seen you I have endeavoured often 'to

reason against the reasons of my love.' I can do that
no more, the pain would be too great.   My love is
selfish; I cannot breathe without you."

(II.)

[Date uncertain—say towards June 15, 1820.]

"MY DEAREST FANNY,—My head is puzzled this
morning, and I scarce know what I shall say, though
I am full of a hundred things.   'Tis certain I would
rather be writing to you this morning, notwithstanding
the alloy of grief in such an occupation, than enjoy any
other pleasure, with health to boot, unconnected with you.
Upon my soul I have loved you to the extreme.   I wish
you could know the tenderness with which I continually
brood over your different aspects of countenance, action,
and dress.   I see you come down in the morning; I see
you meet me at the window; I see everything over again
eternally that I ever have seen.   If I get on the pleasant
clue, I live in a sort of happy misery; if on the unpleasant, 'tis miserable misery.

"You complain of my ill-treating you in word,
thought, and deed.[1]   I am sorry—at times I feel bitterly
sorry that I ever made you unhappy.   My excuse is that
those words have been wrung from me by the sharpness
of my feelings.   At all events, and in any case, I have
been wrong: could I believe that I did it without any

---

[1] Apparently Miss Brawne had remonstrated against the imputation of "flirting with Brown," and much else to like effect in a
recent letter from Keats.

cause, I should be the most sincere of penitents. I could give way to my repentant feelings now, I could recant all my suspicions, I could mingle with you heart and soul, though absent, were it not for some parts of your letters. Do you suppose it possible I could ever leave you? You know what I think of myself, and what of you : you know that I should feel how much it was my loss, and how little yours.

" 'My friends laugh at you.' I know some of them : when I know them all, I shall never think of them again as friends, or even acquaintance. My friends have behaved well to me in every instance but one ; and there they have become tattlers, and inquisitors into my conduct—spying upon a secret I would rather die than share it with anybody's confidence. For this I cannot wish them well ; I care not to see any of them again. If I am the theme, I will not be the friend of idle gossips. Good gods, what a shame it is our loves should be so put into the microscope of a coterie ! Their laughs should not affect you—(I may perhaps give you reasons some day for these laughs, for I suspect a few people to hate me well enough, *for reasons I know of,* who have pretended a great friendship for me)—when in competition with one who, if he never should see you again, would make you the saint of his memory. These laughers, who do not like you, who envy you for your beauty, who would have God-blessed me from you for ever, who were plying me with discouragements with respect to you eternally ! People are revengeful : do not mind them. Do nothing but love me : if I knew that for certain, life and health will in such event be a heaven, and death itself will be less painful. I long to believe in immortality: I shall never be able to bid you an entire farewell. If I am destined to be happy with you here, how short is the longest life! I wish to believe in immortality—I wish to live with you for ever. Do not let my name ever pass between you and those laughers: if I have no other merit than the great love for you, that were sufficient to keep me sacred and unmentioned in such society. If I have been cruel and unjust, I swear my love has ever been greater than my cruelty—which lasts but a minute, whereas my love, come what will, shall last for ever. If concession to me has hurt your pride, God knows I have had little pride in my heart when thinking of you. Your name never passes my lips—do not let mine pass yours. Those people do not like me.

"After reading my letter, you even then wish to see me. I am strong enough to walk over: but I dare not —I shall feel so much pain in parting with you again. My dearest love, I am afraid to see you: I am strong, but not strong enough to see you. Will my arm be ever round you again, and, if so, shall I be obliged to leave you again?

"My sweet love, I am happy whilst I believe your first letter. Let me be but certain that you are mine heart and soul, and I could die more happily than I could otherwise live. If you think me cruel, if you think I have slighted you, do muse it over again, and see into my heart. My love to you is 'true as truth's simplicity, and simpler than the infancy of truth'—as I think I once said before. How could I slight you? how threaten to leave you? Not in the spirit of a threat to you—no, but in the spirit of wretchedness in myself. My fairest, my delicious, my angel Fanny, do not believe me such a vulgar fellow. I will be as patient in illness and as believing in love as I am able."

(III.)

(This is the last letter of the series. Its date is un-certain; but may, as already intimated, be towards July 10, 1820. It follows next after our No. 2.)

"MY DEAREST GIRL,—I wish you could invent some means to make me at all happy without you. Every hour I am more and more concentrated in you; every-thing else tastes like chaff in my mouth. I feel it almost impossible to go to Italy. The fact is, I cannot leave you, and shall never taste one minute's content until it pleases chance to let me live with you for good. But I will not go on at this rate. A person in health, as you are, can have no conception of the horrors that nerves and a temper like mine go through.

"What island do your friends propose retiring to? I should be happy to go with you there alone, but in company I should object to it: the backbitings and jealousies of new colonists, who have nothing else to amuse themselves, is unbearable. Mr. Dilke came to see me yesterday, and gave me a very great deal more pain than pleasure. I shall never be able any more to endure the society of any of those who used to meet at

Elm Cottage [1] and Wentworth Place. The last two years
taste like brass upon my palate. If I cannot live with
you, I will live alone.

" I do not think my health will improve much while I
am separated from you. For all this, I am averse to
seeing you : I cannot bear flashes of light, and return into
my glooms again. I am not so unhappy now as I should
be if I had seen you yesterday. To be happy with you
seems such an impossibility : it requires a luckier star
than mine—it will never be.

" I enclose a passage from one of your letters which I
want you to alter a little : I want (if you will have it so)
the matter expressed less coldly to me.

" If my health would bear it, I could write a poem
which I have in my head, which would be a consolation
for people in such a situation as mine. I would show
some one in love, as I am, with a person living in such
liberty as you do. [2] Shakespeare always sums up matters
in the most sovereign manner. Hamlet's heart was full of
such misery as mine is, when he said to Ophelia, 'Go to a
nunnery, go, go !' Indeed, I should like to give up the
matter at once—I should like to die. I am sickened at
the brute world you are smiling with. I hate men, and
women more. I see nothing but thorns for the future :

---

[1] I observe this name occurring once elsewhere in relation to
Keats, but am not clear whose house it represents.

[2] It has been suggested (by Dante Gabriel Rossetti, as printed in
Mr. Forman's edition of Keats) that the poem here referred to is
" The Eve of St. Mark." Keats had begun it fully a year and a
half before the date of this letter, but, not having continued it, he
might have spoken of " having it in his head."

wherever I may be next winter, in Italy or nowhere, Brown
will be living near you, with his indecencies. I see no
prospect of any rest. Suppose me in Rome. Well, I
should there see you, as in a magic glass, going to and from
town at all hours——I wish I could infuse a little confidence of human nature into my heart : I cannot muster
any. The world is too brutal for me. I am glad there
is such a thing as the grave—I am sure I shall never
have any rest till I get there. At any rate, I will indulge
myself by never seeing any more Dilke or Brown or any
of their friends. I wish I was either in your arms full of
faith, or that a thunderbolt would strike me.—God bless
you. "J. K."

It is seldom one reads a letter (not to speak of a love-
letter) more steeped than this in wretchedness and acrimony ; wretchedness for which the cause was but too real
and manifest; acrimony for which no ground has been
shown or is to be surmised. What Mr. Dilke had done,
or could be supposed to have done, to merit the invalid's
ire, is unapparent. Mr. Brown may be inferred, from
the verses of Keats already quoted, to have had the
general character and bearing of a *bon vivant* or "jolly
dog"; sufficiently versed in the good things of this world,
whether fish, flesh, or womankind; jocose, or on
occasion slangy. But Keats himself, in the nearly contemporary letter in which he arraigned Miss Brawne for
"flirting with Brown," had said : "I know his love and
friendship for me—at this moment I should be without
pence were it not for his assistance ;" and we refuse to
think that any contingency could be likely to arise in

which his "indecencies" would put Miss Brawne to the
blush.   Be it enough for us to know that Keats, in the
drear prospect of expatriation and death, wrote in this
strain, and to wish it were otherwise.

The time had now arrived when Keats was to go to
Italy.   It was on the 18th of September 1820 that he
embarked on the *Maria Crowther* from London. Haydon
gives us a painful glimpse of the poet shortly before his
departure : " The last time I saw him was at Hampstead,
lying on his back in a white bed, helpless, irritable, and
hectic.   He had a book, and, enraged at his own feeble-
ness, seemed as if he were going out of the world, with a
contempt of this, and no hopes of a better.   He mut-
tered as I stood by him that, if he did not recover, he
would ' cut his throat.'   I tried to calm him, but to no
purpose.   I left him, in great depression of spirit to see
him in such a state."   Another attached friend, of whom
I have not yet made mention, accompanied him ; and in
the annals of watchful and self-oblivious friendship there
are few records more touching than the one which links
with the name of John Keats that of Joseph Severn.
Severn, two years older than Keats, had known him as far
back as 1813, being introduced by Mr. William Haslam.
Keats was then studying at Guy's Hospital, but none the
less gave Severn "the complete idea of a poet."   The
acquaintance does not seem to have proceeded far at
that date ; but, through the intervention of Mr. Edward
Holmes (author of a " Life of Mozart," and " A Ramble
among the Musicians of Germany ") was renewed whilst
the poet was composing " Endymion" ; and Severn may
probably have co-operated in some minor degree with

Haydon in training Keats to a perception of the great things in plastic art. In 1820 Severn, a student-painter at the Royal Academy, had won the gold medal by his picture of The Cave of Despair, from Spenser, entitling him to the expenses of a three years' stay in Italy, for advancement in his art. He had an elegant gift in music, as well as in painting; and it is a satisfaction to learn that at this period he had "great animal spirits," for without these what he went through during the ensuing five months would have been but too likely to break him down. I must make room here for another letter from Keats, one addressed to his good friend Brown, deeply pathetic, and serving to assuage whatever may have been like "brass upon our palate" in the last-quoted letter to Fanny Brawne.

" *Saturday, September* 28.
" *Maria Crowther*, off Yarmouth, Isle of Wight.

"MY DEAR BROWN,—The time has not yet come for a *pleasant* letter from me. I have delayed writing to you from time to time, because I felt how impossible it was to enliven you with one heartening hope of my recovery. This morning in bed the matter struck me in a different manner. I thought I would write ' while I was in some liking,' or I might become too ill to write at all, and then, if the desire to have written should become strong, it would be a great affliction to me. I have many more letters to write, and I bless my stars that I have begun, for time seems to press—this may be my best opportunity.

. "We are in a calm, and I am easy enough this morning.

If my spirits seem too low you may in some degree impute it to our having been at sea a fortnight without making any way. I was very disappointed at not meeting you at Bedhampton, and am very provoked at the thought of you being at Chichester to-day.[1] I should have delighted in setting off for London for the sensation merely—for what should I do there? I could not leave my lungs or stomach or other worse things behind me.

" I wish to write on subjects that will not agitate me much. There is one I must mention, and have done with it. Even if my body would recover of itself, this would prevent it. The very thing which I want to live most for will be a great occasion of my death. I cannot help it—who can help it? Were I in health, it would make me ill, and how can I bear it in my state? I daresay you will be able to guess on what subject I am harping: you know what was my greatest pain during the first part of my illness at your house. I wish for death every day and night to deliver me from these pains; and then I wish death away, for death would destroy even those pains, which are better than nothing. Land and sea, weakness and decline, are great separators; but death is the great divorcer for ever. When the pang of this thought has passed through my mind, I may say the bitterness of death is past. I often wish for you, that you might flatter me with the best.

[1] This may require a word of explanation. Keats, detained at Portsmouth by stress of weather, had landed for a day, and seen his friend Mr. Snook, at Bedhampton. Brown was then in Chichester, only ten miles off, but of this Keats had not at the time been aware.

"I think, without my mentioning it, for my sake you would be a friend to Miss Brawne when I am dead. You think she has many faults: but for my sake think she has not one. If there is anything you can do for her by word or deed, I know you will do it. I am in a state at present in which woman, merely as woman, can have no more power over me than stocks and stones; and yet the difference of my sensations with respect to Miss Brawne and my sister is amazing. The one seems to absorb the other to a degree incredible. I seldom think of my brother and sister in America. The thought of leaving Miss Brawne is beyond everything horrible—the sense of darkness coming over me—I eternally see her figure eternally vanishing. Some of the phrases she was in the habit of using during my last nursing at Wentworth Place ring in my ears. Is there another life? Shall I awake and find all this a dream? There must be—we cannot be created for this sort of suffering. The receiving this letter is to be one of yours.

" I will say nothing about our friendship, or rather yours to me, more than that, as you deserve to escape, you will never be so unhappy as I am. I should think of—you [1] in my last moments. I shall endeavour to write to Miss Brawne if possible to-day.[2] A sudden

[1] The — before "you" appears in the letter, as printed in Mr. Forman's edition of Keats. It might seem that Keats hesitated a moment whether to write "you" or "Miss Brawne."

[2] No such letter is known. It has been stated that Keats, after leaving home, could never summon up resolution enough to write to Miss Brawne: possibly this statement ought to be limited to the time after he had reached Italy.

stop to my life in the middle of one of these letters would be no bad thing, for it keeps one in a sort of fever awhile.

"Though fatigued with a letter longer than any I have written for a long while, it would be better to go on for ever than awake to a sense of contrary winds. We expect to put into Portland Roads to-night. The captain, the crew, and the passengers are all ill-tempered and weary. I shall write to Dilke. I feel as if I was closing my last letter to you."

The ship at last proceeded on her voyage, and in the Bay of Biscay encountered a severe squall. Keats soon afterwards read the storm-scene in Byron's "Don Juan": he threw the book away in indignation, denouncing the author's perversity of mind which could "make solemn things gay, and gay things solemn." Late in October he reached the harbour of Naples, and had to perform a tedious quarantine of ten days. After landing on the 31st,[1] he received a second letter from Shelley, then at Pisa, urging him to come to that city. The first letter

---

[1] Lord Houghton says that Keats in Naples "could not bear to go to the opera, on account of the sentinels who stood constantly on the stage:" he spoke of "the continual visible tyranny of this government," and said "I will not leave even my bones in the midst of this despotism." Sentinels on the stage have, I believe, been common in various parts of the continent, as a mere matter of government parade, or of routine for preserving public order. The other points (for which no authority is cited by Lord Houghton) must, I think, be over-stated. In November 1820 the short-lived constitution of the kingdom of Naples was in full operation, and neither tyranny nor despotism was in the ascendant—rather a certain degree of popular license.

on this subject, dated in July, had invited Keats to the
hospitality of Shelley's own house; but in November
this project had been given up, as "we are not rich
enough for that sort of thing"—although Shelley still
intended (so he wrote to Leigh Hunt) "to be the
physician both of his body and his soul,—to keep the
one warm, and to teach the other Greek and Spanish."
Keats, however, had brought with him a letter of introduction to Dr. (afterwards Sir James) Clark, in Rome,—
or indeed he may have met him before leaving England
—and he decided to proceed to Rome rather than Pisa.
Dr. Clark engaged for him a lodging opposite his own:
it was in the first house on the right as you ascend the
steps of the Trinità del Monte. The precise date when
Keats reached Rome, his last place of torture and of
rest, does not appear to be recorded: it was towards the
middle of November. He was at first able to walk out
a little, and occasionally to ride. Dr. Clark attended
his sick bed with the most exemplary assiduity and kindness. He pronounced (so Keats wrote to Brown in a
letter of November 30th, which is perhaps the last he
ever penned) that the lungs were not much amiss, but
the stomach in a very bad condition: perhaps this was a
kindly equivocation, for by this time—as was ascertained
after his death—Keats can have had scarcely any lungs
at all. The patient was under no illusion as to his
prospects, and he more than once asked the physician
"When will this posthumous life of mine come to an
end?"

The only words in which the last days of Keats can
be adequately recorded are those of Severn: our best

choice would be between extract and silence. There were oscillations from time to time, from bad to less bad; but generally the tendency of the disease was steadily downwards. The poet's feelings regarding Fanny Brawne were so acute and harrowing that he never mentioned her to his friend. I give a few particulars from Severn's contemporary letters—the person addressed being not always known.

"*December* 14. His suffering is so great, so continued, and his fortitude so completely gone, that any further change must make him delirious.

"*December* 17. Not a moment can I be from him. I sit by his bed and read all day, and at night I humour him in all his wanderings. . . . He rushed out of bed and said 'This day shall be my last,' and but for me most certainly it would. The blood broke forth in similar quantity the next morning, and he was bled again. I was afterwards so fortunate as to talk him into a little calmness, and he soon became quite patient. Now the blood has come up in coughing five times. Not a single thing will he digest, yet he keeps on craving for food. Every day he raves he will die from hunger, and I've been obliged to give him more than was allowed. . . . Dr. Clark will not say much. . . . All that can be done he does most kindly; while his lady, like himself in refined feeling, prepares all that poor Keats takes, for —in this wilderness of a place for an invalid—there was no alternative.

[To Mrs. Brawne.]   "*January* 11. He has now given up all thoughts, hopes, or even wish, for recovery.

His mind is in a state of peace, from the final leave he
has taken of this world, and all its future hopes. . . . I
light the fire, make his breakfast, and sometimes am
obliged to cook; make his bed, and even sweep the
room. . . . Oh I would my unfortunate friend had never
left your Wentworth Place for the hopeless advantages of
this comfortless Italy ! He has many many times talked
over 'the few happy days at your house, the only time
when his mind was at ease'. . . . Poor Keats cannot
see any letters—at least he will not; they affect him so
much, and increase his danger. The two last I repented
giving : he made me put them into his box, unread.

"*January* 15. Torlonia the banker has refused us
any more money. The bill is returned unaccepted, and
to-morrow I must pay my last crown for this cursed
lodging-place : and what is more, if he dies, all the beds
and furniture will be burnt, and the walls scraped, and
they will come on me for a hundred pounds or more.
. . . You see my hopes of being kept by the Royal
Academy will be cut off unless I send a picture in the
spring. I have written to Sir T. Lawrence.

"*February* 12. At times I have hoped he would
recover; but the doctor shook his head, and Keats would
not hear that he was better; the thought of recovery is
beyond everything dreadful to him.

[To Mrs. Brawne.] "*February* 14. His mind is
growing to great quietness and peace. I find this
change has its rise from the increasing weakness of his
body; but it seems like a delightful sleep to me, I have
been beating about in the tempest of his mind so long.
To-night he has talked very much to me, but so easily

that he at last fell into a pleasant sleep. He seems to have comfortable dreams without nightmare. This will bring on some change : it cannot be worse—it may be better. Among the many things he has requested of me to-night, this is the principal—that on his grave. shall be this, 'Here lies one whose name was writ in water.' . . . Such a letter has come ! I gave it to Keats, supposing it to be one of yours; but it proved sadly otherwise. The glance of that letter tore him to pieces. The effects were on him for many days. He did not read it—he could not; but requested me to place it in his coffin, together with a purse and letter (unopened) of his sister's : since which time he has requested me not to place *that* letter in his coffin, but only his sister's purse and letter, with some hair. Then he found many causes of his illness in the exciting and thwarting of his passions; but I persuaded him to feel otherwise on this delicate point. . . . I have got an English nurse to come two hours every other day. . . . He has taken half a pint of fresh milk : the milk here is beautiful to all the senses—it is delicious. For three weeks he has lived on it, sometimes taking a pint and a half in a day.

"*February* 22. This morning, by the pale daylight, the change in him frightened me : he has sunk in the last three days to a most ghastly look. . . . He opens his eyes in great doubt and horror ; but, when they fall upon me, they close gently, open quietly, and close again, till he sinks to sleep.

"*February* 27. He is gone. He died with the most perfect ease—he seemed to go to sleep. On the 23rd, about four, the approaches of death came on. 'Severn

—I—lift me up. I am dying—I shall die easy. Don't be frightened : be firm, and thank God it has come.' I lifted him up in my arms. The phlegm seemed boiling in his throat, and increased until eleven, when he gradually sank into death, so quiet that I still thought he slept. I cannot say more now. I am broken down by four nights' watching, no sleep since, and my poor Keats gone. Three days since the body was opened : the lungs were completely gone. The doctors could not imagine how he had lived these two months. I followed his dear body to the grave on Monday [February 26th], with many English. . . . The letters I placed in the coffin with my own hand."

No words of mine shall be added here to tarnish upon the mirror of memory this image of a sacred death and a sacred friendship.

CHAPTER IV

W E have now reached the close of a melancholy history—that of the extinction, in a space of less than twenty-six years, of a bright life foredoomed by inherited disease. We turn to another subject—the intellectual development and the writings of Keats, what they were, and how they were treated. Here again there are some sombre tints.

A minute anecdote, apparently quite authentic, shows that a certain propensity to the jingle of rhyme was innate in Keats: Haydon is our informant. "An old lady (Mrs. Grafty, of Craven Street, Finsbury) told his brother George—when, in reply to her question what John was doing, he told her he had determined to become a poet—that this was very odd; because when he could just speak, instead of answering questions put to him, he would always make a rhyme to the last word people said, and then laugh." This, however, is the only rhyming-anecdote that we hear of Keats's childhood or mere boyhood: there is nothing to show that at school he made the faintest attempt at verse-spinning. The earliest known experiment of his is the "Imitation of Spenser"—four Spenserian stanzas, beginning—

" Now Morning from her orient chamber came,"

and very poor stanzas they are. This Imitation was
written while he was living at Edmonton, in his nineteenth
year, and thus there was nothing singularly precocious in
Keats, either in the age at which he began versifying, or
in the skill with which he first addressed himself to the
task. I might say more of other verses, juvenile in the
amplest sense of the term, but such remarks would
belong more properly to a later section of this volume.
I will therefore only observe here that the earliest poems
of his in which I can discern anything even distantly
approaching to poetic merit or to his own characteristic
style (and these distantly indeed) are the lines "To ——"

" Hadst thou lived in days of old,"

and " Calidore, a Fragment,"

" Young Calidore is paddling o'er the lake."

The dates of these two compositions are not stated, but
they were probably later than the opening of 1815, and
if so Keats would have been nearly or quite twenty when
he wrote them—and this is far remote from precocity.
Let us say then, once for all, that, whatever may be the
praise and homage due to Keats for ranking as one of
the immortals when he died aged twenty-five, no sort of
encomium can be awarded to him on the ground that,
when he first began, he began early and well. All his
rawest attempts, be it added to his credit, appear to have
been kept to himself; for Cowden Clarke, who was certainly his chief literary confidant in those tentative days,
says that until Keats produced to him his sonnet

5

"written on the day that Mr. Leigh Hunt left prison" the youth's attempts at verse-writing were to him unknown. The 3rd of February 1815 was the day of Hunt's liberation, so that the endeavour had by this time been going on in silence for something like a year or more.

It was not till 1816—or let us say when he was just of age—that Keats produced a truly excellent thing. This is the sonnet "On first looking into Chapman's Homer." A copy of Chapman's translation had been lent to Cowden Clarke; he and Keats sat up till daylight reading it, the young poet shouting with delight, and by ten o'clock on the following morning Keats sent the sonnet to Clarke. It was therefore a sudden immediate inspiration, a little rill of lava flowing out of a poetic volcano, solidified at once. This is not only the first excellent thing written by Keats—it is the *only* excellent thing contained in his first volume of verse.

This volume came out (as already mentioned) in the early spring of 1817. The sonnet dedicating the book to Leigh Hunt, written off at a moment's notice "when the last proof-sheet was brought from the printer," was evidently composed in winter-time. The title of the volume is "Poems by John Keats." The motto on its title-page is from Spenser—

"What more felicity can fall to creature
Than to enjoy delight with liberty?"

—a motto embodying with considerable completeness the feeling which is predominant in the volume, and generally in Keats's poetic works. We always feel "delight" to

be his true element, whatever may be the undertone of
pathos opposed to it by poetic development and treatment, and by adverse fate. " Liberty " also—a free
flight of the faculties, a rejection of conventional
trammels, whether in life or in verse—was highly
characteristic of him ; and perhaps the youthful friend of
Hunt intended the word "liberty" to be understood by
his readers as having a certain political flavour as well.
In addition to some writings just specified, the volume
contained "I stood tiptoe upon a little hill " ; the
three epistles "To George Felton Mathew" (who was a
gentleman of literary habits, afterwards employed in
administering the Poor Law), "To my brother George,"
and " To Charles Cowden Clarke "; sixteen sonnets; and
"Sleep and Poetry." The question of the poetic deserv-
ings of these compositions belongs more properly to our
final chapter. I shall here give only a few details bearing
upon the circumstances of their production. The poem
"I stood tiptoe " &c. was written beside a gate near Caen
Wood, Highgate. It must have been begun in a summer,
no doubt that of 1816, and was still uncompleted in the
middle of December of that year. " The Epistle to
Mathew," dated November 1815, testifies to the early
admiration of Keats for Thomas Chatterton ; though the
dedication of " Endymion," "Inscribed to the memory of
Thomas Chatterton," was but poorly forestalled by such
lines as the following—

" Where we may soft humanity put on,
   And sit and rhyme, and think on Chatterton,
   And that warm-hearted Shakspeare sent to meet him
   Four laurelled spirits heavenward to entreat him."

Moreover, the first of his youthful sonnets is addressed to Chatterton.   The " Epistle to George," August 1816, opens with a reference to "many a dreary hour " which John Keats has passed, fearing he would never be able to write good poetry, however much he might gaze on sky, honey-bees, and the beauty of woman.   The " Epistle to Clarke," September 1816, pays ample tribute to the guidance which he had afforded to Keats into the realms of poetry, and contains a couplet which has of late been very often quoted—

> " Who read for me the sonnet swelling loudly
>   Up to its climax, and then dying proudly ? "

The sonnet—

> "O Solitude, if I must with thee dwell,"

is the first thing that Keats ever published.   It had previously appeared in *The Examiner* for May 5, 1816, and is clearly one of the best of these early sonnets.   The sonnet which begins with the unmetrical line—

> " How many bards gild the lapses of time "

was included in the very first batch of verses by Keats which Cowden Clarke showed to Leigh Hunt.   Hunt expressed "unhesitating and prompt admiration " of some other one among the compositions ; and Horace Smith, who was present, reading out the sonnet now before us, praised as "a well-condensed expression " the contorted and inefficient line—

> "That distance of recognizance bereaves,"

i.e. [sounds] which distance bereaves of recognizance, or, in plain English, which are too distant to be recognized. Two other sonnets are addressed to Haydon in a tone of glowing laudation.

"Sleep and Poetry " is (if we except the sonnet upon Chapman's Homer) by far the most important poem in the volume. It was written partly in Leigh Hunt's cottage at Hampstead, in the library-room, where a sofa-bed had on one occasion been made up for Keats's convenience, and the latter lines in the poem refer to objects of art which were kept in the room. Apart from the impressive line which all readers remember, saying of poetry—

> " 'Tis might half-slumbering on its own right arm,"

there are several passages interesting as showing Keats's enthusiasm for the art in which he was now a beginner, soon to be an adept—

> " Oh for ten years that I may overwhelm
> Myself in poesy ! "

also

> " The great end
> Of poesy, that it should be a friend
> To soothe the cares and lift the thoughts of man ; "

and again

> " They shall be accounted poet-kings
> Who simply tell the most heart-easing things "—

both of these being definitions in which we might imagine Leigh Hunt to have borne his part, or at least notified his concurrence. The following well-known diatribe is also important, and should be kept in mind when we come to speak of the reception accorded to Keats by established critics, more or less of the old school. He has been dilating on the splendours of British poetry of the great era, say Spenser to Milton, and then proceeds—

> " Could all this be forgotten ?   Yes, a schism
> Nurtured by foppery and barbarism
> Made great Apollo blush for this his land.
> Men were thought wise who could not understand
> His glories : with a puling infant's force
> They swayed about upon a rocking-horse,
> And thought it Pegasus.   Ah dismal-souled !
> The winds of heaven blew, the ocean rolled
> Its gathering waves—ye felt it not ; the blue
> Bared its eternal bosom, and the dew
> Of summer-night collected still to make
> The morning precious.   Beauty was awake—
> Why were ye not awake ?   But ye were dead
> To things ye knew not of—were closely wed
> To musty laws lined out with wretched rule
> And compass vile ; so that ye taught a school
> Of dolts to smoothe, inlay, and chip, and fit,
> Till—like the certain wands of Jacob's wit—
> Their verses tallied.   Easy was the task ;
> A thousand handicraftsmen wore the mask
> Of Poesy.   Ill-fated impious race,
> That blasphemed the bright lyrist to his face,
> And did not know it !   No, they went about
> Holding a poor decrepit standard out
> Marked with most flimsy mottoes, and in large
> The name of one Boileau."

Zeal is generally pardonable.   Keats's was manifestly

honest zeal, and flaming forth in the right direction. Yet it would have been well for him to remember and indicate that amid his "school of dolts," bearing the flag of Boileau, there had been some very strong and capable men, notably Dryden and Pope, who could do several things besides inlaying and clipping; nor could it be said that the beauty of the world had been wholly blinked by so pre-eminently descriptive a poet as Thomson; and, if we were to read Boileau—which few of us do now-a-days, and I daresay Keats was not one of the few—we should probably find that his "mottoes" were much less concerned with inlaying and clipping than with solid meaning and studious congruity—qualities not totally contemptible, but (be it acknowledged) very largely contemned by Keats in that first slender performance of his adolescence named "Poems, 1817."

It has been said that this volume hardly went beyond the circle of Keats's personal friends; nor do I think this statement can be far wrong, although one inquirer avers that the book was "constantly alluded to in the prominent periodicals." The dictum of Keats himself stands thus : "It was read by some dozen of my friends, who liked it ; and some dozen whom I was unacquainted with, who did not." Shelley cannot have been among the friends who liked the volume, for he had recommended Keats not to give it to the press. At any rate the publishers, Messrs. Ollier, would after a very short while sell it no more. Their letter to George Keats—who seems to have been acting for John during the absence of the latter in the Isle of Wight or at Margate—is too amusing to be omitted :—

"We regret that your brother ever requested us to publish his book, or that our opinion of its talent should have led us to acquiesce in undertaking it. We are, however, much obliged to you for relieving us from the unpleasant necessity of declining any further connexion with it, which we must have done, as we think the curiosity is satisfied and the sale has dropped. By far the greater number of persons who have purchased it from us have found fault with it in such plain terms that we have in many cases offered to take the book back rather than be annoyed with the ridicule which has time after time been showered upon it. In fact, it was only on Sunday last that we were under the mortification of having our own opinion of its merits flatly contradicted by a gentleman who told us he considered it 'no better than a take-in.' These are unpleasant imputations for any one in business to labour under ; but we should have borne them and concealed their existence from you had not the style of your note shown us that such delicacy would be quite thrown away. We shall take means without delay for ascertaining the number of copies on hand, and you shall be informed accordingly.

"3 Welbeck Street, 29th April 1817."

I do not find that the after-fate of the "Poems" is recorded : probably they were handed over to Messrs. Taylor and Hessey, who undertook the publication of "Endymion."

CHAPTER V

T O "Endymion" we now have to turn. The early verses of Keats (as well as the later ones) contain numerous allusions to Grecian mythology—Muses, Apollo, Pan, Narcissus, Endymion and Diana, &c. For the most part these early allusions are nothing more than tawdry conventionalisms; so indeed are some of the later ones, as for instance in the drama of "King Stephen," written in 1819, the schoolboy classicism of "2nd Captain"—

> " Royal Maud
> From the thronged towers of Lincoln hath looked down,
> Like Pallas from the walls of Ilion ; "

and we cannot discover that any more credit is due to Keats for dribbling out his tritenesses about Apollo and the Muses than to any Akenside, Mason, or Hayley, of them all. At times, however, there is a genuine tone of *enjoyment* in these utterances sufficient to persuade us that the subject had really taken possession of his mind, and that he could feel Grecian mythology, not merely as a convenient vehicle for rhetorical personifications, but as an ever-vital embodiment of ideas of beauty in forms of beauty. In the early and partly boyish poem, "I stood

tip-toe upon a little hill," a good deal of space is devoted
to showing that classical myths are an outcome of eager
sensitiveness to the lovely things of Nature°: the tales of
Psyche, Pan and Sirynx, Narcissus, are cited in confir-
mation—and finally Diana and Endymion, in the following lines :—

" Where had he been from whose warm head outflew
    That sweetest of all songs, that ever new,
    That aye-refreshing pure deliciousness
            Coming ever to bless
    The wanderer by moonlight ? to him bringing
    Shapes from the invisible world, unearthly singing
    From out the middle air, from flowery nests,
    And from the pillowy silkiness that rests
    Full in the speculation of the stars.
    Ah surely he had burst our mortal bars :
    Into some wondrous region he had gone
    To search for thee, divine Endymion.
    He was a poet, sure a lover too,
    Who stood on Latmus' top what time there blew
    Soft breezes from the myrtle-vale below,
    And brought—in faintness solemn, sweet, and slow—
    A hymn from Dian's temple, while upswelling
    The incense went to her own starry dwelling.
    But, though her face was clear as infants' eyes,
    Though she stood smiling o'er the sacrifice,
    The poet wept at her so piteous fate—
    Wept that such beauty should be desolate ;
    So in fine wrath some golden sounds he won,
    And gave meek Cynthia her Endymion.
    Queen of the wide air, thou most lovely queen
    Of all the brightness that mine eyes have seen,
    As thou exceedest all things in thy shine,
    So every tale does this sweet tale of thine.
    Oh for three words of honey that I might
    Tell but one wonder of thy bridal night !

Where distant ships do seem to show their keels
Phœbus awhile delayed his mighty wheels,
And turned to smile upon thy bashful eyes
Ere he his unseen pomp would solemnize.

＊　　＊　　＊　　＊　　＊

Cynthia, I cannot tell the greater blisses
That followed thine and thy dear shepherd's kisses :
Was there a poet born ? "

Readers often go at a skating-pace over passages of this kind, without very clearly realizing to themselves the gist of the whole matter. I will therefore put the thing into the most prosaic form, and say that what Keats substantially intimates here is as follows :—The inventor of the myth of Artemis and Endymion must have been a poet and lover, who, standing on the hill of Latmos, and hearing thence a sweet hymn wafted from the low-lying temple of Artemis, while the pure maiden-like moon was shining resplendently, felt a pang of pity for this loveless moon or Artemis, and invented for her a lover in the person of Endymion ; and ever since then the myth has lent additional beauty to the effects, beautiful as in themselves they are, of moonlight. Without tying down Keats too rigidly to this view of the genesis of the myth, I may nevertheless point out that he wholly ignores as participants both the spirit of religious devoutness, and the device of allegorizing natural phænomena : the inventor is simply a poet and lover, who thinks it a world of pities that such a sweet maiden as Artemis should not have a lover sooner or later. Invention prompted by warmth of feeling is thus the sole motive-power recognized. The final phrase " Was there a poet born ? " may without violence be understood as implying, " Ought not the loves of Artemis and Endymion to beget their poet, and why should not I be that poet ? " At all events, Keats determined that he *would* be that poet ; and, contemplating the original invention of the myth from the point of view which we have just analysed, he not unnaturally treated it from a like point of view. The tale of Diana and Endymion was not to be a monument of classic antiquity re-stated in the timid, formal spirit of a school-exercise, but an invention of a poet and lover, who, acting under the spell of natural beauty, re-informs his theme with poetic fancy, amorous ardour, and Nature's profusion of object and of imagery. And in this Keats thought—and surely he rightly thought—that he would be getting closer to the spirit of a Grecian myth than by any cut-and-dry process of tame repetition or pulseless decorum. He wanted the dell of wild flowers, and not the *hortus siccus.*

"Endymion" was actually begun in the spring of 1817, much about the same time when the volume " Poems " was published. The first draft was completed (as we have said) on the 28th of November 1817, and by the end of the winter which opened the year 1818 no more probably remained to be done to it. The MS. was subjected to much revision and excision, so that it cannot be alleged that Keats worked in a reckless temper, or without such self-criticism as he could at that date bring to bear. It would even appear, moreover, from the terms of a letter which he addressed to Mr. Taylor, on April 27, 1818, that he allowed that gentleman to make some volunteer corrections of his own. Haydon had spurred him on to

the ambitious attempt, which Hunt on the contrary depre-
cated. Shelley—so the story goes—agreed with Keats
that each of them should write an epic within a space of
six months. Shelley produced "The Revolt of Islam,"
Keats the "Endymion." Shelley proved to be the more
rapid writer of the two ; for his poem of 4815 lines was
finished by the early autumn of 1817, while Keats's,
numbering 4,050 lines, went on through the winter which
opened 1818. A good deal of it had been done during
Keats's sojourn with Mr. Bailey, in Magdalen Hall,
Oxford. Afterwards, on 8th October 1817, he wrote to
Bailey—" I refused to visit Shelley, that I might have
my own unfettered scope ;" an expression which one
might be inclined to understand as showing that Shelley,
having now completed " The Revolt of Islam," had invited
Keats to visit him at Marlow, and there to proceed with
" Endymion,"—not without the advantage it may well be
supposed, of Shelley's sympathizing but none the less
stringent counsel. Bailey's account of the facts may
be given here. "He wrote and I read—sometimes
at the same table, sometimes at separate desks—
from breakfast till two or three o'clock. He sat down to
his task, which was about fifty lines a day, with his paper
before him, and wrote with as much regularity and
apparently with as much ease as he wrote his letters.
Indeed, he quite acted up to the principle he lays down,
'That, if poetry comes not as naturally as the leaves of a
tree, it had better not come at all.' Sometimes he fell
short of his allotted task, but not often, and he would
make it up another day. But he never forced himself.
When he had finished his writing for the day, he usually

read it over to me, and then read or wrote letters till we
went out for a walk." The first book of the poem was
delivered into the hands of the publisher, Mr. Taylor, in
the middle of January. Haydon undertook to make a
finished chalk-sketch of the author's head, to be prefixed
to the volume ; he drew outlines accordingly, but the
volume, an octavo, appeared in April without any portrait.
We all know the now proverbial first line in "Endymion,"

"A thing of beauty is a joy for ever."

This seems to have been an inspiration of long anterior
date ; for Mr. Stephens, the surgical fellow-student and
fellow-lodger of Keats, says that in one twilight when they
were together the youthful poet produced the line—

"A thing of beauty is a constant joy ; "

which, failing wholly to satisfy its author's ear, was immediately afterwards improved into its present form.
Even before handing over any part· of his MS. to the
printer, Keats, at the " immortal dinner " which came off
in Haydon's painting-room, on the 28th of December
1817, and at which Wordsworth, Lamb, and others, were
present, had bespoken a strange and heroic fate for one
copy of his book ; for he made Mr. Ritchie, who was
about to set forth on an African exploration, promise
that he would carry the volume " to the great desert of
Sahara, and fling it in the midst."

"Invention" was the quality which Keats most sought
for in his "Endymion," as shown in his letter to Mr.
Bailey, already cited. He said—" It ['Endymion'] will

be a test of my powers of imagination, and chiefly of my invention—which is a rare thing indeed—by which I must make 4000 lines of one bare circumstance, and fill them with poetry. . . . A long poem is a test of Invention, which I take to be the polar star of poetry, as Fancy is the sails, and Imagination the rudder. . . . This same Invention seems indeed of late years to have been forgotten as a poetical excellence." The term "invention" might be used in various senses. Keats seems to have meant the power of producing a great number of minor incidents, illustrative images, and other particulars, all tending to reinforce and fill out the main conception and subject-matter.

Keats wrote a preface to "Endymion" on March 19, 1818, which was objected to by Hamilton Reynolds, and by his friends generally. It was certainly off-hand and unconciliating, and some readers would have regarded it as defiant. Its general purport was that the poem was faulty, but the author would not keep it back for revision, which would make the performance a tedium to himself, "I have written to please myself, and in hopes to please others, and for a love of fame." There was a good deal more, jaunty and provocative enough. Keats was not well inclined to suppress this preface. He replied on April 9th to Reynolds in a letter from which some weighty words must be quoted :—

"I have not the slightest feeling of humility towards the public, or to anything in existence but the Eternal Being, the principle of Beauty, and the memory of great men. . . . A preface is written to the public—a thing

I cannot help looking upon as an enemy, and which
I cannot address without feelings of hostility. . . . I
would be subdued before my friends, and thank them
for subduing me; but among multitudes of men I have
no feel of stooping—I hate the idea of humility to them.
I never·wrote one single line of poetry with the least
shadow of public thought. . . . I hate a mawkish popu-
larity. I cannot be subdued before them. My glory
would be to daunt and dazzle the thousand jabberers
about pictures and books."

Keats, however, yielded to his censors, and wrote a
rather shorter preface, by far a better one. It bears the
date of April 10th, being the very next day after he had
written to Reynolds in so unsubmissive a tone. This
second preface says substantially much the same thing as
the first, but without any aggressive or " devil-may-care"
addenda. It is too important to be omitted here :—

" Knowing within myself the manner in which this
poem has been produced, it is not without a feeling of
regret that I make it public. What manner I mean will
be quite clear to the reader, who must soon perceive
great inexperience, immaturity, and every error denoting a
feverish attempt rather than a deed accomplished. The
two first books, and indeed the two last, I feel sensible,
are not of such completion as to warrant their passing
the press ; nor should they, if I thought a year's castigation would do them any good. It will not: the founda-
tions are too sandy. It is just that this youngster should
die away—a sad thought for me, if I had not some hope

that, while it is dwindling, I may be plotting, and fitting myself for verses fit to live.

"This may be speaking too presumptuously, and may deserve a punishment. But no feeling man will be forward to inflict it; he will leave me alone with the conviction that there is not a fiercer hell than the failure in a great object. This is not written with the least atom of purpose to forestall criticisms of course, but from the desire I have to conciliate men who are competent to look, and who do look, with a zealous eye to the honour of English literature.

" The imagination of a boy is healthy, and the mature imagination of a man is healthy. But there is a space of life between in which the soul is in a ferment, the character undecided, the way of life uncertain, the ambition thick-sighted. Thence proceeds mawkishness, and all the thousand bitters which those men I speak of must necessarily taste in going over the following pages.

"I hope I have not in too late a day touched the beautiful mythology of Greece, and dulled its brightness; for I wish to try once more before I bid it farewell."

No one can deny that this is a modest preface; it is in fact too modest, and concedes to the adversary the utmost which could possibly be at issue, viz., whether the poem was worth publishing or not. The only scintilla of self-assertion in it is the hope expressed—"*some* hope" —that the writer might eventually produce "verses fit to live;" and less than that no man who puts a poem before the public could be expected to postulate. Keats must therefore be expressly acquitted of having done anything

6

to excite animosity or retaliation on the part of his critics;
the sole thing which could be attacked was the poem
itself—too frankly pronounced indefensible—or else something in the author which did not appear within the
covers of his volume.   The preface is indeed manly as
well as modest; there is not a servile or obsequious word
in it; yet I cannot help thinking that Keats, when later
on he found "Endymion" denounced as drivel, must at
times have wished that he had been a little less deferen-
tial to Reynolds's objections, and had not so explicitly
admitted that not one of the four books of the poem was
qualified to "pass the press."   An adverse reviewer was
sure to take advantage of that admission, and did so.

It would be interesting to compare with the preface
which Keats printed for "Endymion" the one which
Shelley printed for "The Revolt of Islam."   Shelley, like
Keats, was modest; he left his readers to settle any question as to his poetic claims (although "Alastor," previously published, might pretty well have vouched
for these); but he resolutely explained that reviewers
would find in him no subject for bullying.   I can only
make room for a few sentences :—

"The experience and the feelings to which I refer do
not in themselves constitute men poets, but only prepare
them to be the auditors of those who are.   How far I
shall be found to possess that more essential attribute of
poetry, the power of awakening in others sensations like
those which animate my own bosom, is that which, to
speak sincerely, I know not, and which, with an acqui-
escent and contented spirit, I expect to be taught by the

effect which I shall produce upon those whom I now
address. . . . It is the misfortune of this age that its
writers, too thoughtless of immortality, are exquisitely
sensible to temporary praise or blame. They write with
the fear of reviews before their eyes. This system of
criticism sprang up in that torpid interval when poetry
was not. Poetry, and the art which professes to regulate
and limit its powers, cannot subsist together. . . . I have
sought, therefore, to write (as I believe that Homer,
Shakespeare, and Milton wrote) in utter disregard of
anonymous censure."

The publisher of "Endymion" (Mr. Taylor is probably
meant) was nervous as to the reception which potent
critics would accord to the volume. He went to William
Gifford, the editor of the *Quarterly Review*, to bespeak
indulgence, but found a Cerberus who rejected every sop.
In the number of the *Quarterly* for April 1818—not
actually published, it would seem, until September—
appeared a critique branded into ignominious perma-
nence by the name and fame of Keats. Gifford himself
is regarded as its author. As an account of Keats's
career would for various reasons be incomplete in the
absence of this critique, I reproduce it here. It has the
merit of brevity, and lends itself hardly at all to curtail-
ment, but I miss one or two details, relating chiefly to
Leigh Hunt.

"Reviewers have been sometimes accused of not
reading the works which they affected to criticize. On
the present occasion we shall anticipate the author's
complaint, and honestly confess that we have not read

his work. Not that we have been wanting in our duty; far from it; indeed, we have made efforts, almost as super-human as the story itself appears to be, to get through it: but, with the fullest stretch of our perseverance, we are forced to confess that we have not been able to struggle beyond the first of the four books of which this Poetic Romance consists. We should extremely lament this want of energy, or whatever it may be, on our parts, were it not for one consolation—namely, that we are no better acquainted with the meaning of the book through which we have so painfully toiled than we are with that of the three which we have not looked into.

"It is not that Mr. Keats (if that be his real name, for we almost doubt that any man in his senses would put his real name to such a rhapsody)—it is not, we say, that the author has not powers of language, rays of fancy, and gleams of genius. He has all these ; but he is un-happily a disciple of the new school of what has been somewhere called 'Cockney Poetry,' which may be defined to consist of the most incongruous ideas in the most uncouth language.

"Of this school Mr. Leigh Hunt, as we observed in a former number, aspires to be the hierophant. . . . This author is a copyist of Mr. Hunt, but he is more unintelligible, almost as rugged, twice as diffuse, and ten times more tiresome and absurd, than his prototype, who, though he impudently presumed to seat himself in the chair of criticism, and to measure his own poetry by his own standard, yet generally had a meaning. But Mr. Keats had advanced no dogmas which he was bound to support by examples. His nonsense, therefore, is quite gratuitous; he writes it for its own sake, and, being bitten by Mr. Leigh Hunt's insane criticism, more than rivals the insanity of his poetry.

"Mr. Keats's preface hints that his poem was produced under peculiar circumstances. 'Knowing within myself,' he says, 'the manner [&c., down to 'a deed accomplished']. We humbly beg his pardon, but this does not appear to us to be 'quite so clear;' we really do not know what he means. But the next passage is more intelligible. 'The two first books, and indeed the two last, I feel sensible, are not of such completion as to warrant their passing the press.' Thus 'the two first books' are, even in his own judgment, unfit to appear, and 'the two last' are, it seems, in the same condition; and, as two and two make four, and as that is the whole number of books, we have a clear, and we believe a very just, estimate of the entire work.

"Mr. Keats, however, deprecates criticism on this 'immature and feverish work' in terms which are themselves sufficiently feverish; and we confess that we should have abstained from inflicting upon him any of the tortures of the 'fierce hell' of criticism [1] which terrify his imagination if he had not begged to be spared in order that he might write more; if we had not observed in him

---

[1] The reader of Keats's preface will note that this is a misrepresentation. Keats did not speak of any fierce hell of criticism, nor did he ask to remain uncriticized in order that he might write more. What he said was that a feeling critic would not fall foul of him for hoping to write good poetry in the long run, and would be aware that Keats's own sense of failure in "Endymion" was as fierce a hell as he could be chastised by.

a certain degree of talent which deserves to be put in the right way, or which at least ought to be warned of the wrong ; and if finally he had not told us that he is of an age and temper which imperiously require mental discipline.

"Of the story we have been able to make out but little. It seems to be mythological, and probably relates to the loves of Diana and Endymion ; but of this, as the scope of the work has altogether escaped us, we cannot speak with any degree of certainty, and must therefore content ourselves with giving some instances of its diction and versification. And here again we are perplexed and puzzled. At first it appeared to us that Mr. Keats had been amusing himself and wearying his readers with an immeasurable game at *bouts rimés*; but, if we recollect rightly, it is an indispensable condition at this play that the rhymes, when filled up, shall have a meaning ; and our author, as we have already hinted, has no meaning. He seems to us to write a line at random, and then he follows, not the thought excited by this line, but that suggested by the *rhyme* with which it concludes. There is hardly a complete couplet enclosing a complete idea in the whole book. He wanders from one subject to another, from the association, not of ideas, but of sounds ; and the work is composed of hemistichs which, it is quite evident, have forced themselves upon the author by the mere force of the catchwords on which they turn.

"We shall select, not as the most striking instance, but as that least liable to suspicion, a passage from the opening of the poem.

'Such the sun, the moon,
Trees old and young, sprouting a shady boon
For simple sheep ; and such are daffodils,
With the green world they live in ; and clear rills
That for themselves a cooling covert make
'Gainst the hot season ; the mid-forest brake
Rich with a sprinkling of fair musk-rose blooms ;
And such too is the grandeur of the dooms
We have imagined for the mighty dead,' &c.

Here it is clear that the word, and not the idea, *moon*, produces the simple sheep and their shady *boon*, and that 'the *dooms* of the mighty dead' would never have intruded themselves but for the ' fair musk-rose *blooms*.'

"Again—

' For 'twas the morn.   Apollo's upward fire
Made every eastern cloud a silvery pyre
Of brightness so unsullied that therein
A melancholy spirit well might win
Oblivion, and melt out his essence fine
Into the winds.   Rain-scented eglantine
Gave temperate sweets to that well-wooing sun ;
The lark was lost in him ; cold springs had run
To warm their chilliest bubbles in the grass ;
Man's voice was on the mountains : and the mass
Of Nature's lives and wonders pulsed tenfold
To feel this sunrise and its glories old.'

Here Apollo's *fire* produces a *pyre*—a silvery pyre—of clouds, *wherein* a spirit might *win* oblivion, and melt his essence *fine* ; and scented *eglantine* gives sweets to the *sun*, and cold springs had *run* into the *grass ;* and then the pulse of the *mass* pulsed *tenfold* to feel the glories *old* of the new-born day, &c.

"One example more—

> ' Be still the unimaginable lodge
> For solitary thinkings, such as dodge
> Conception to the very bourne of heaven,
> Then leave the naked brain ; be still the leaven
> That, spreading in this dull and clodded earth,
> Gives it a touch ethereal—a new birth.'

Lodge, dodge—heaven, leaven—earth, birth—such, in six words, is the sum and substance of six lines.

"We come now to the author's taste in versification. He cannot indeed write a sentence, but perhaps he may be able to spin a line. Let us see. The following are specimens of his prosodial notions of our English heroic metre :

> ' Dear as the temple's self, so does the moon,
> The passion poesy, glories infinite.

> ' So plenteously all weed-hidden roots.

> ' Of some strange history, potent to send.

> ' Before the deep intoxication.

> ' Her scarf into a fluttering pavilion.

> ' The stubborn canvas for my voyage prepared.

> ' Endymion, the cave is secreter
> Than the isle of Delos. Echo hence shall stir
> No sighs but sigh-warm kisses, or light noise
> Of thy combing hand, the while it travelling cloys
> And trembles through my labyrinthine hair.'

"By this time our readers must be pretty well satisfied as to the meaning of his sentences and the structure of his lines. We now present them with some of the new words with which, in imitation of Mr. Leigh Hunt, he adorns our language.

"We are told that turtles *passion* their voices; that an arbour was *nested*, and a lady's locks *gordianed* up; and, to supply the place of the nouns thus verbalized, Mr. Keats, with great fecundity, spawns new ones, such as men-slugs and human *serpentry*, the *honey-feel* of bliss, wives prepare *needments*, and so forth.

"Then he has formed new verbs by the process of cutting off their natural tails, the adverbs, and affixing them to their foreheads. Thus the wine out-sparkled, the multitude up-followed, and night up-took; the wind up-blows, and the hours are down-sunken. But, if he sinks some adverbs in the verbs, he compensates the language with adverbs and adjectives which he separates from the parent stock. Thus a lady whispers *pantingly* and close, makes *hushing* signs, and steers her skiff into a *ripply* cove, a shower falls *refreshfully*, and a vulture has a *spreaded* tail.

"But enough of Mr. Leigh Hunt and his simple neophyte. If any one should be bold enough to pur-chase this 'Poetic Romance,' and so much more patient than ourselves as to get beyond the first book, and so much more fortunate as to find a meaning, we entreat him to make us acquainted with his success. We shall then return to the task which we now abandon in despair, and endeavour to make all due amends to Mr. Keats and to our readers."

Such is the too famous article in *The Quarterly Review*. If its contents are to be assessed with perfect calmness,

I should have to say that it is not mistaken in alleging
that the poem of "Endymion" is rambling and indistinct;
that Keats allowed himself to drift too readily according
to the bidding of his rhymes (Leigh Hunt has acknow--
ledged as much, in independent remarks of his own);
that many words are coined, and badly coined ; and that
the versification is not free from blemishes—although·
several of the lines quoted by *The Quarterly* as unmetrical,.
are, when read with the right emphasis, blameless, or even.
sonorous.   But the article is none the less a despicable·
and odious performance ; partly as being a sneering
depreciation of a work showing rich poetic endowment,
and partly as being, not a deliberate and candid (however·
severe) estimate of Keats as a poet, but really an utterance of malice prepense, and hardly disguised, against
Hunt as a hostile politician who wrote poetry, and against.
any one who consorted with him.   The inverting of the
due balance between the merits and the defects of
" Endymion," would have been at best an act of stupidity ;.
at second best, after the author's preface had been laid
to heart, an act of brutalism ; and at worst, when the
venom of abuse was poured into the poetic cup of Keats
as an expedient for drugging the political cup of Hunt,.
an act of partisan turpitude.   No more words need be
wasted upon a proceeding of which the abiding and un-
evadeable literary record is graven in the brass of
Shelley's " Adonais."

The attack in *The Quarterly Review* was accompanied
by attacks in *Blackwood's Magazine.*   If *The Quarterly*
was carping and ill-natured, *Blackwood* was basely insult-
ing.   A series of articles " On the Cockney School of

Poetry" began in the Scotch magazine in October
1817, being directed mainly, and with calumnious viru-
lence, against Leigh Hunt. No. 4 of the series came
out in August 1818, and formed a vituperation of
Keats. I will not draw upon its stores of underbred
jocularity, so as to show that the best raillery which
Blackwood could get up consisted of terming him
Johnny Keats, and referring to his having been
assistant to an "apothecary." The author of these
papers signed himself Z, being no doubt too noble and
courageous to traduce people without muffling himself in
anonymity; nor did he consent to uncloak, though
vigorously pressed by Hunt to do so. It is affirmed that
Z was Lockhart, the son-in-law of Sir Walter Scott, and
afterwards editor of *The Quarterly Review ;* and an unpleasant adjunct to this statement—we would gladly
disbelieve it—is that Scott himself lent active aid in con-
cocting the articles. A different account is that Z was at
first John Wilson (Christopher North), revised by William.
Blackwood, but that the article on Keats was due to
Lockhart.

Few literary questions of the last three-quarters of a
century have been regarded from more absolutely different
points of view than the problem—How did Keats
receive the attacks made upon his poem and himself?
From an early date in the controversy three points seem
to have been very generally agreed upon: (1) That
"Endymion" is (as Shelley judiciously phrased it), "a
poem considerably defective;" (2) that the attacks upon
it were, in essence, partly true, but so biassed—so keen of
scent after defects, and so dull of vision for beauties—as

to be practically unfair and perverse in a marked degree ;
and (3) that the unfairness and perversity *quoad* Keats
were wilful devices of literary and especially of political
spite *quoad* a knot of writers among whom Leigh Hunt
was the central figure.   The question remains—In what
spirit did Keats meet his critics?   Was he greatly dis-
tressed, or defiant and retaliatory, or substantially indifferent ?

Among the documents of Keats's life I find few records
strictly contemporary with the events themselves, serving
to settle this point.   When the abuse of Z against Hunt
began, Keats was indignant and combative.   He said in
a letter which may belong to October 1817—

"There has been a flaming attack upon Hunt in the
Edinburgh magazine. . . . There has been but one
number published—that on Hunt, to which they have
prefixed a motto by one Cornelius Webb, 'Poetaster,'
who unfortunately was one of our party occasionally at
Hampstead, and took it into his head to write the following (something about)—

> 'We'll talk on Wordsworth, Byron,
> A theme we never tire on,'

and so forth till he came to Hunt and Keats.   In the
motto they have put 'Hunt and Keats' in large letters.
I have no doubt that the second number was intended
for me, but have hopes of its non-appearance. . . . I
don't mind the thing much ; but, if he should go to such
lengths with me as he has done with Hunt, I must infallibly call him to an account, if he be a human being,

and appears in squares and theatres where we might
'possibly meet.' I don't relish his abuse."

It is worth observing also that, in a paper "On Kean.
as Richard Duke of York" which Keats published on.
December 28, 1817, he wrote : " The English people do
not care one fig about Shakespeare, only as he flatters
their pride and their prejudices ; . . . it is our firm.
opinion." If he thought that English indifference to
Shakespeare was of this degree of density, he must surely
have been prepared for a considerable amount of apathy
in relation to any poem by John Keats.

On October 9, 1818, just after the spiteful notices of
himself in *Blackwood* and *The Quarterly* had appeared,
and had been replied to in *The Morning Chronicle* by
two correspondents signing J. S. and R. B., Keats wrote
as follows to his publisher Mr. Hessey ; and to treat the
affair in a more self-possessed, measured, and dignified
spirit, would not have been possible :—

" You are very good in sending me the letters from
The Chronicle, and I am very bad in not acknowledging
such a kindness sooner ; pray forgive me. It has so
chanced that I have had that paper every day. I have
seen to-day's. I cannot but feel indebted to those gen-
tlemen who have taken my part. As for the rest, I begin
to get a little acquainted with my own strength and weakness. Praise or blame has but a momentary effect on the
man whose love of beauty in the abstract makes him a
severe critic on his own works. My own domestic
criticism has given me pain without comparison beyond
what *Blackwood* or *The Quarterly* could possibly inflict ;

and also, when I feel I am right, no external praise can give me such a glow as my own solitary reperception and ratification of what is fine. J. S. is perfectly right in regard to the 'slipshod " Endymion." '[1] That it is so is no fault of mine. No; though it may sound a little paradoxical, it is as good as I had power to make it by myself. Had I been nervous about its being a perfect piece, and with that view asked advice, and trembled over every page, it would not have been written, for it is not in my nature to fumble. I will write independently. I have written independently, *without judgment:* I may write independently, and *with judgment*, hereafter. The genius of poetry must work out its own salvation in a man. It cannot be matured by law and precept, but by sensation and watchfulness in itself. That which is creative must create itself. In 'Endymion' I leaped headlong into the sea, and thereby have become better acquainted with the soundings, the quicksands, and the rocks, than if I had stayed upon the green shore and piped a silly pipe, and took tea and comfortable advice. I was never afraid of failure, for I would sooner fail than not be among the greatest. But I am nigh getting into a rant ; so, with remembrances to Taylor and Woodhouse, &c., I am yours very sincerely,

"JOHN KEATS."

This letter, equally moderate and wide-reaching, proves conclusively that Keats, at the time when he wrote it, treated depreciatory criticism in exactly the right spirit;

---

[1] This phrase stands printed with inverted commas, as a quotation. It is not, however, a quotation from the letter of J. S.

acknowledging that it was not without a certain *raison
d'être*, but affirming that he could for himself see much
further and much deeper in the same direction, and in
others as well. On October 29, 1818, he wrote to his
brother George :—

"Reynolds . . . persuades me to publish my ' Pot of
Basil' as an answer to the attack made on me in *Blackwood's Magazine* and *The Quarterly Review.* . . . I think
I shall be among the English poets after my death. Even
as a matter of present interest, the attempt to crush me
in *The Quarterly* has only brought me more into notice,
and it is a common expression among book-men, 'I
wonder *The Quarterly* should cut its own throat.' It
does me not the least harm in society to make me appear
little and ridiculous. I know when a man is superior to
me, and give him all due respect; he will be the last to
laugh at me; and as for the rest, I feel that I make an
impression upon them which ensures me personal respect
while I am in sight, whatever they may say when my back
is turned. . . . The only thing that can ever affect me
personally for more than one short passing day is any
doubt about my powers for poetry. I seldom have any;
and I look with hope to the nighing time when I shall
have none."

Towards December 1818 he wrote in a similarly contented strain to George Keats and his wife : "You will
be glad to hear that Gifford's attack upon me has done
me service; it has got my book among several *sets.*" The
same letter mentions a sonnet, and a bank-note for £25

received from an unknown admirer. However, the next letter to the same correspondents, February 19, 1819, clearly attests some annoyance.

"My poem has not at all succeeded. . . . The reviewers have enervated men's minds, and made them indolent ; few think for themselves. These reviews are getting more and more powerful, especially *The Quarterly*. They are like a superstition which, the more it prostrates the crowd and the longer it continues, the more it becomes powerful, just in proportion to their increasing weakness. I was in hopes that, as people saw (as they must do now), all the trickery and iniquity of these plagues, they would scout them. But no ; they are like the spectators at the Westminster cockpit ; they like the battle, and do not care who wins or who loses. . . . I have been at different times turning it in my head whether I should go to Edinburgh and study for a physician. . . . It is not worse than writing poems, and hanging them up to be fly-blown in the Review shambles."

We find in Keats's letters nothing further about the criticisms ; but, when he replied in August 1820 to Shelley's first invitation to Italy, he referred to "Endymion" itself : "I am glad you take any pleasure in my poor poem, which I would willingly take the trouble to unwrite if possible, did I care so much as I have done about reputation." We must also take into account the publishers' advertisement (not Keats's own) to the "Lamia" volume, saying of "Hyperion"—"The poem was intended to have been of equal length with 'Endymion,' but the reception given to that work discouraged the author from proceeding." It can scarcely be supposed that the publishers printed this without Keats's express sanction; yet he never assigned elsewhere any similar reason for discontinuing "Hyperion," nor was "Hyperion" open to exception on any such grounds as had been urged against "Endymion."

The earliest written reference which I can trace to any serious despondency of Keats consequent upon the attacks of reviewers (if we except a less strongly worded statement by Leigh Hunt, to be quoted further on) is in a letter which Shelley wrote, but did not eventually send, to the editor of the *Quarterly Review*. It was written after Shelley had seen the "Lamia" volume, and can hardly, I suppose, date earlier than October 1820, two full years after the publication of the *Quarterly* (and also the *Blackwood*) tirades against "Endymion." Shelley adverts, with great reserve of tone, to the *Quarterly* critique, and then proceeds—

"Poor Keats was thrown into a dreadful state of mind by this review, which I am persuaded was not written with any intention of producing the effect (to which it has at least greatly contributed) of 'embittering his existence, and inducing a disease from which there are now but faint hopes of his recovery. The first effects are described to me to have resembled insanity, and it was by assiduous watching that he was restrained from effecting purposes of suicide. The agony of his sufferings at length produced the rupture of a blood-vessel in the lungs, and the usual process of consumption appears to have begun."

The informants of Shelley with regard to Keats's acute feelings and distress were (it is stated) the Gisbornes, and possibly Leigh Hunt may have confirmed them in some measure; but the Gisbornes knew nothing directly of what had been taking place in England in or about the autumn of 1818, and that which Hunt published regarding Keats is far from corroborating so extreme a view of the facts. Later on Shelley received from Mr. Gisborne a letter written by Colonel Finch, the date of which would perhaps be in May 1821 (three months after the death of Keats). This letter appears to have been one of his principal incentives for the indignation expressed in the preface to " Adonais," but not in the poem itself, which had been completed before Shelley saw the letter; and it is remarkable that Colonel Finch's expressions, when one scrutinizes them, do not really say anything about mental anguish caused to Keats by any review, but only by ill-treatment of a different kind— seemingly that of his brother George and others, as previously detailed. The following is the only relevant passage : " He left his native shores by sea in a merchant vessel for Naples, where he arrived, having received no benefit during the passage, and brooding over the most melancholy and mortifying reflections, and nursing a deeply-rooted disgust to life and to the world, owing to having been infamously treated by the very persons whom his generosity had rescued from want and woe." Shelley however put into print in the preface to " Adonais " the same view of the blighting of Keats's life by the *Quarterly* critique (he seems to have known nothing of the *Blackwood* scurrility), which had appeared in his undespatched letter to the editor of the *Quarterly*—

"The savage criticism on his 'Endymion' which appeared in *The Quarterly Review* produced the most violent effect on his susceptible mind. The agitation thus originated ended in the rupture of a blood-vessel in the lungs. A rapid consumption ensued, and the succeeding acknowledgments from more candid critics of the true greatness of his powers were ineffectual to heal the wound thus wantonly inflicted. . . . Miserable man! you, one of the meanest, have wantonly defaced one of the noblest specimens of the workmanship of God. Nor shall it be your excuse that, murderer as you are, you have spoken daggers but used none."

Thus far we have found no strong evidence (only assertions) that Keats took greatly to heart the attacks upon him, whether in the *Quarterly* or in *Blackwood*. Shelley seems to be the principal authority, and Shelley, unless founding upon some adequate information, is next to no authority at all. He had left England in March 1818, five months before the earlier—printed in August— of these spiteful articles. Were there nothing further, we should be more than well pleased to rally to the opinion of Lord Houghton, who came to the conclusion that the idea of Keats's extreme sensitiveness to criticism was a positive delusion—that he paid little heed to it, and pursued his own course much as if no reviewer had tried to be provoking. But there is, in fact, a direct witness of high importance—Haydon. Haydon knew Keats very intimately, and saw a great deal of him ; he admired and loved him, and had a vigorous, discerning insight into character and habit of mind, such as makes his observa-

tions about all sorts of men substantial testimony and
first-rate reading. He took forcible views of many
things, and sometimes exaggerated views : but, when he
attributed to Keats a particular mood of feeling, I should
find it very difficult to think that he was either unfairly
biassed or widely mistaken. In his reminiscences
proper to the year 1817–18 occurs the following
passage :—

" The assaults on Hunt in *Blackwood* at this time,
under the signature of Z, were incessant. Who Z was
nobody knew, but I myself strongly suspect him to have
been Terry the actor. Leigh Hunt had exasperated
Terry by neglecting to notice his theatrical efforts. Terry
was a friend of Sir Walter's, shared keenly his political
hatreds, and was also most intimate with the Blackwood
party, which had begun a course of attacks on all who
showed the least liberalism of thinking, or who were
praised by or known to *The Examiner*. Hunt had
addressed a sonnet to me. This was enough : we were
taken to be of the same clique of rebels, rascals, and
reformers, who were supposed to support that production
of so much power and talent. On Keats the effect was
melancholy. He became morbid and silent; would call
and sit whilst I was painting, for hours, without speaking
a word."

This counts for something—not very much. But
another passage forming an entry in Haydon's diary,
written on March 29, 1821, perhaps as soon as he had
heard of Keats's death, carries the matter much further—

"He began life full of hopes, fiery, impetuous, and ungovernable, expecting the world to fall at once beneath his powers. Poor fellow! his genius had no sooner begun to bud than hatred and malice spat their poison on its leaves, and, sensitive and young, it shrivelled beneath their effusions. Unable to bear the sneers of ignorance or the attacks of envy, not having strength of mind enough to buckle himself together like a porcupine and present nothing but his prickles to his enemies, he began to despond, and flew to dissipation as a relief, which, after a temporary elevation of spirits, plunged him into deeper despondency than ever. For six weeks he was scarcely sober, and (to show what a man does to gratify his appetites when once they get the better of him) once covered his tongue and throat as far as he could reach with cayenne pepper in order to appreciate the 'delicious coldness[1] of claret in all its glory '—his own expression."

Immediately afterwards, April 21, 1821, Haydon wrote a letter to Miss Mitford, repeating, with some verbal variations, what is said above, and adding several other particulars concerning Keats. The opening phrase runs thus : " Keats was a victim to personal abuse, and want of nerve to bear it. Ought he to have sunk in that way because a few quizzers told him that he was an apothecary's apprentice ? " And further on—" I remonstrated on his absurd dissipation, but to no purpose." The reader will observe that this dissipation, six weeks of insobriety, is alleged to have occurred after Keats

---

[1] " Coolness " (which seems to be the right word) in the letter to Miss Mitford.

" began to despond." The precise time when he began
to despond is not defined, but we may suppose it to have
been in the late autumn of 1818. If so, it was much
about the same period when he first made Miss Brawne's
acquaintance.

It is true that Mr. Cowden Clarke, when he published
certain " Recollections " in *The Gentleman's Magazine* in
1874, strongly contested these statements of Haydon's ;
he disbelieved the cayenne pepper and the dissipation,
and had " never perceived in Keats even a tendency to
imprudent indulgence." The " Recollections " were
afterwards reproduced as a volume, and in the volume
the confutation of Haydon disappeared ; whether because
Clarke had eventually changed his opinion, or for what
other reason, I am unable to say. Anyhow, Haydon's
evidence remains ; it relates to a period of Keats's life
when Haydon no doubt saw him much oftener than
Clarke did, and we must observe that he refers to
" Keats's own expression " as to the claret ensuing after
the cayenne pepper, and affirms that he himself remonstrated in vain against the " dissipation," which means
apparently excess in drinking alone.

To advert to what Lord Byron wrote about Keats as
having been killed by *The Quarterly Review* is hardly
worth while. His first reference to the subject is in a
letter to Mr. Murray (publisher of *The Quarterly*) dated
April 26, 1821. In this he expressly names Shelley as
his informant, and with Shelley as an authority for the
allegation I have already dealt.

There are two writings of Leigh Hunt in which the
question of Keats and his critics is touched upon. The

first is the review, August 1820, of the "Lamia" volume. In speaking of the " Ode to a Nightingale " he says—

" The poem will be the more striking to the reader when he understands, what we take a friend's liberty in telling him, that the author's powerful mind has for some time past been inhabiting a sickened and shaken body; and that in the meanwhile it has had to contend with feelings that make a fine nature ache for its species, even when it would disdain to do so for itself—we mean critical malignity, that unhappy envy which would wreak its own tortures upon others, especially upon those that really feel for it already."

Hunt's posthumous Memoir of Keats was first published in 1828. He refers to the attack in *Blackwood* upon himself and upon Keats, and says: " I little suspected, as I did afterwards, that the hunters had struck him; that a delicate organization, which already anticipated a premature death, made him feel his ambition thwarted by these fellows; and that the very impatience of being impatient was resented by him and preyed on his mind." Hunt also says regarding Byron—" I told him he was mistaken in attributing Keats's death to the critics, though they had perhaps hastened and certainly embittered it."

Another item of evidence may be cited. It is from a letter written by George Keats to Mr. Dilke in April 1824, and refers to the insolences of *Blackwood's Magazine.* George, it will be remembered, was already out of England before the articles appeared in *Blackwood*

and in *The Quarterly*, and he only saw a little of John
Keats at the close of the ensuing year, 1819. "*Blackwood's Magazine* has fallen into my hands.   I could
have walked 100 miles to have dirked him *à l'Améri-
caine* for his cruelly associating John in the Cockney
School, and other blackguardisms.   Such paltry ridicule
will have wounded deeper than the severest criticisms,
particularly as he regarded what is called the cockneyism
of the coterie with so much disgust.   He either knew
John well, and touched him in the tenderest place pur-
posely; or knew nothing of him, and supposed he went
all lengths with the set in their festering opinions and
cockney affectations."   And from a later letter dated in
April 1825 : "After all, *Blackwood* and *The Quarterly*,
associated with our family disease, consumption, were
ministers of death sufficiently venomous, cruel, and
deadly, to have consigned one of less sensibility to a
premature grave. . . . John was the very soul of courage
and manliness, and as much like the Holy Ghost as
'Johnny Keats.'"

The evidence of latest date on this subject (there is
none such in Severn's correspondence [1]) is that of
Cowden Clarke.   In his "Recollections," already mentioned, he refers to the attacks upon Keats, having his
eye, it would seem, rather upon those in *Blackwood* than
in *The Quarterly*, and he remarks : "To say that these
disgusting misrepresentations did not affect the conscious-

---

[1] Severn's view of the matter some years afterwards has however
received record in the diary of Henry Crabb Robinson.   Under the
date May 6, 1837, we read—"He [Severn] denies that Keats's
death was hastened by the article in the *Quarterly*."

ness and self-respect of Keats would be to under-rate the sensitiveness of his nature. He did feel and resent the insult, but far more the *injustice* of the treatment he had received. They no doubt had injured him in the most wanton manner; but, if they or my Lord Byron ever for one moment supposed that he was crushed or even cowed in spirit by the treatment he had received, never were they more deluded."

I have now given all the evidence at first or second hand which seems to be producible on that much-vexed question—Was Keats (to adopt Byron's phrase) "snuffed out by an article"? The upshot appears to me to be as follows. In his inmost mind Keats was from first to last raised very far above that level where the petty gales of review-criticism blow, puffing out the canvas of feeble reputations, and fraying that of strong ones. Nevertheless he was sensitive to derisive criticism, and more especially to personal ridicule, and even (as Haydon records) gave way to his feelings of irritation with reckless and culpable self-abandonment. This passed off partially, and would have passed off entirely—it has left in his letters no trace worth mentioning, and in his poetry no trace at all, other than that of executive power braced up to do constantly better and yet better; but then, about a year and a half after the reviews, supervened his fatal illness (which cannot be reasonably supposed to have had its root in any critiques), and all the heartache of his unsatisfied love. This last formed the real agony of his waning life: it must have been reinforced to some extent by resentment against a mode of reviewing which would contribute to the thwarting of his poetic ambition, and make him go

down into the grave with a " name writ in water ; " but the
reviews themselves counted for very little in the last
wrestlings of his spirit with death and nothingness.   By
general constitution of mind few men were less adapted
than Keats for being "snuffed out by an article," or
more certain to snuff one out and leave all its ill-savour
to its scribe.

CHAPTER VI

THE first important poem to which Keats sets his hand after finishing "Endymion" was "Isabella, or The Pot of Basil." This was completed by April 27, 1818, the same month in which "Endymion" was published. Hamilton Reynolds had suggested the project of producing a volume of tales in verse, founded upon stories in Boccaccio's "Decameron"; some of the tales would have been executed by Reynolds himself, who did in fact produce on this plan the two poems named collectively "The Garden of Florence." As it turned out, however, Keats's tale appeared in a volume of his own, 1820, and Reynolds's two came out independently in the succeeding year.

"The Eve of St. Agnes" was written in the winter beginning the year 1819. Then came "Hyperion," of which two versions remain, both fragmentary. The first version (begun perhaps as early as October or September 1818), the only one which Keats himself published, is in all respects by far the better. He was much under the spell of Milton while he wrote it; and finally he gave it up in September 1819, declaring that "there were too many Miltonic inversions in it." He went so

far as to say in a letter written in the same month that
"the 'Paradise Lost,' though so fine in itself, is a cor-
ruption of our language—a northern dialect accommo-
dating itself to Greek and Latin inversions and
intonations." "Hyperion" was included in Keats's
third volume at the request of the publishers, contrary
to the author's own preference. One may readily infer
that it was to "Hyperion" that he referred when, in the
preface to "Endymion," he spoke of returning to
Grecian mythology for another subject: the full length
of the poem was to have been ten books.

"Lamia" was the last poem of considerable length
which Keats brought to completion and published. It
seems to have been begun towards the summer of 1819,
and was written with great care, after a heedful study of
Dryden's methods of composition. On September 18,
1819, Keats wrote: "I am certain there is that sort of
fire in it which must take hold of people in some way,
give them either pleasant or unpleasant sensations." The
subject was taken from Burton's "Anatomy of Melancholy," in which there is a reference to the "Life of
Apollonius" by Philostratus as the original source of the
legend.

The volume—entitled "Lamia, Isabella, The Eve of
St. Agnes, and other Poems"—came out towards the
beginning of July 1820, when the malady of Keats had
reached an advanced and alarming stage. At the beginning of September Keats wrote to Brown—"The sale
of my book is very slow, though it has been very highly
rated." I am not aware that there is any other record
to show how far the publication may ultimately have

approached towards becoming a commercial success; nor indeed would it be altogether easy to define the date at which Keats became a recognized and uncontested poet of high rank, and his works a solid property. His early death, at the beginning of 1821, must have formed a turning-point—not to speak of the favourable notice of "Endymion," and subordinately of the "Lamia" volume, which appeared in *The Edinburgh Review*, Jeffrey being the critic, in August 1820. Perhaps Jeffrey's praise may have facilitated an arrangement which Keats made in September 1820—the sale of the copyright of "Endymion" to Messrs Taylor and Hessey for £100; no second edition of the poem appeared, however, while he was alive. I should presume that, within five or six years after Keats's decease, ridicule and rancour were already much in the minority; and that, by some such date as 1835 to 1840, they had finally "hidden their diminished heads," living only, with too persistent a life, in the retributive memory of men.

Some of the shorter poems in the "Lamia" volume must receive brief mention here. The "Ode to Psyche" was written in February 1819, and was termed by Keats the first poem with which he had taken pains—"I have for the most part dashed off my lines in a hurry." "To Autumn," the "Ode on Melancholy," and the "Ode on a Grecian Urn," succeeded. The "Ode to a Nightingale" was composed at Hampstead in the spring of 1819 *after breakfast*, forming two or three hours' work: thus we see that the nocturnal imagery of the ode was a general or a particular reminiscence, not actual to the very moment of composition. This poem and the "Ode on a Grecian Urn" were recited by Keats to Haydon in a chaunting tone in Kilburn meadows, and were published in the serial entitled "Annals of the Fine Arts." The urn thus immortalized may probably be one preserved in the garden of Holland House.

With the "Lamia" volume we have come to the close of what Keats published during his lifetime. Something remains to be said of other writings of his—almost all of them earlier in date than the publication of that volume —which remained unprinted or uncollected at the time of his death.

In Feburary 1818 Keats, Leigh Hunt, and Shelley, undertook to write a sonnet each upon the river Nile. In order of merit, the three sonnets are the reverse of what one might have been willing to forecast. I at least am clearly of opinion that Hunt's sonnet is the best (though with a weak ending), Keats's the second, and Shelley's a decidedly bad third. The leading thought in each sonnet is characteristic of its author. Keats adheres to the simple natural facts of the case, while Hunt and Shelley turn the Nile into a moral or intellectual symbol. Keats says essentially that to asso- ciate the Nile with ideas of antique desolation is but a delusion of ignorance, for this river is really rich and fresh like others. Hunt makes the Egyptian stream an emblem of history tending towards the progress of the individual and the race; while Shelley reads into the Nile a lesson of the good and the evil inhering in knowledge.

" The Eve of St. Mark "—a fragment which very few of Keats's completed poems can rival in point of artist-like feeling and writing—belongs to the years 1818–9. I find nothing in print to account for his leaving it un-finished.

In May 1819 Keats had an idea of inventing a new structure of sonnet-rhyme; and he sent to his brother and sister-in-law a sonnet composed accordingly, be-ginning—

" If by dull rhymes our English must be chained."

He wrote: " I have been endeavouring to discover a better sonnet-stanza than we have. The legitimate does not suit the language well, from the pouncing rhymes. The other appears too elegiac, and the couplet at the end of it has seldom a pleasing effect. I do not pretend to have succeeded." Keats's experiment reads agree-ably. It comprises five rhymes altogether; the first rhyme being repeated thrice at arbitrary intervals; and the last rhyme twice in lines twelve and fourteen.

The tragedy of " Otho the Great " was written by Keats (as already referred to) in July and August 1819, in co-operation with Armitage Brown. The diction of the play is, it would appear, Keats's entirely; whereas the invention and development of plot in the first four acts is wholly due to Brown. The two friends sat together; Brown described each successive scene, and Keats turned it into verse, without troubling his head as to the subject-matter for the scene next ensuing. When it came to the fifth act, however, Keats inquired what would be the conclusion of the play; and, not being satisfied with Brown's project which he deemed too humorous and too melodramatic, he both invented and wrote a fifth act for himself. He felt sure that "Otho the Great" was "a tolerable tragedy," and set his heart upon getting it acted—Kean was well inclined to take the principal character, Prince Ludolph ; and it became his greatest ambition to write fine plays. "Otho" was in fact accepted for Drury Lane Theatre, on the offer of Brown, who left Keats's authorship in the background ; but, as both the writers were impatient of delay, Brown, in February 1820, took away the MS., and Covent Garden Theatre was thought of instead—without any practical result. As soon as "Otho" was finished, Brown suggested King Stephen as the subject of another drama ; and Keats, without any further collaboration from his friend, composed the few scenes of it which remain. "One of my ambitions" (writes Keats to Bailey in August 1819), "is to make as great a revolution in modern dramatic writing as Kean has done in acting."

The ballad "La Belle Dame sans Merci," than which Keats did nothing more thrilling or more perfect, may perhaps have been written in the earlier half of 1819 ; it was published in 1820, in Hunt's *Indicator* for May 10th, under the signature "Caviare"; the same signature which was adopted for the sonnet, "A dream, after reading Dante's episode of Paolo and Francesca." Keats may probably have meant to imply, in some bitterness of spirit, that his poems were "caviare to the general." The title of this ballad was suggested to Keats by seeing it at the head of a translation from Alain Chartier in a copy of Chaucer. As to the "Dream" sonnet he wrote in April 1819 :—

"The 5th canto of Dante pleases me more and more ;: it is that one in which he meets with Paulo and Francesca. I had passed many days in rather a low state of mind, and in the midst of them I dreamt of being in that region of Hell. The dream was one of the most delightful enjoyments I ever had in my life. I floated about the wheeling atmosphere, as it is described, with a beautiful figure, to whose lips mine were joined, it seemed for an age ; and in the midst of all this cold and darkness I was warm. Ever-flowery tree-tops sprang up, and we rested on them, sometimes with the lightness of a cloud, till the wind blew us away again. I tried a sonnet on it ; there are fourteen lines in it, but nothing of what I felt. Oh that I could dream it every night !"

The last long work which Keats undertook, and he wrote it with extreme facility, was "The Cap and Bells ; or The Jealousies, a Fairy Tale," in the Spenserian stanza. What remains is probably far less than Keats intended the tale to amount to, but it is enough to enable us to pronounce upon its merits. The poem was begun soon after Keats's first attack of blood-spitting in February 1820. It seems singular that under such depressing conditions he should have written in so frivolous and jaunty a spirit, and provoking that his last long work (the last, that is, if we except the recast of " Hyperion ") should be about the most valueless which he produced, at any date after commencing upon " Endymion." This poem has been said to be written in the spirit of Ariosto ; a statement which, in justice to the brilliant Italian, cannot be admitted. It may well be, however,

8

as Lord Houghton suggests, that the general notion was
suggested by Brown, who had translated the first five
cantos (not indeed of Ariosto, but) of the "Orlando
Innamorato" of Bojardo. "The Cap and Bells"
appears to be destitute of distinct plan, though some
sort of satirical allusion to the marital and extra-marital
exploits of George IV. is traceable in it; meagre and
purposeless in invention; a poor farrago of pumped-up
and straggling jocosity. Perhaps a hearty laugh has
never been got out of it; although there are points here
and there at which a faint snigger may be permissible,
and the concluding portion improves somewhat. Keats
seems to have intended to publish it under a pseudonym,
Lucy Vaughan Lloyd; and Hunt gave, in *The Indicator* of August 23, 1820, some taste of its quality,
possibly meaning to print more of it anon.

The last verses which Keats ever wrote formed the
sonnet here ensuing. He composed this late in September 1820, after landing on the Dorsetshire coast,
probably near Lulworth, and returning to the ship which
bore him to his doom in Italy; and he wrote it down on
a blank page in Shakespeare's Poems, facing "A
Lover's Complaint."

"Bright star, would I were steadfast as thou art ;
    Not in lone splendour hung aloft the night,
And watching with eternal lids apart,
    Like Nature's patient sleepless eremite,
The moving waters at their priestlike task
    Of pure ablution round earth's human shores,
Or gazing on the new soft-fallen mask
    Of snow upon the mountains and the moors :—

No, yet still steadfast, still unchangeable,
  Pillowed upon my fair love's ripening breast,
To feel for ever its soft fall and swell,
  Awake for ever in a sweet unrest ;
Still, still to hear her tender-taken breath,
And so live ever—or else swoon to death."

Of poetic projects which remained unfulfilled when
Keats died we hear—leaving out of count the works
which he had begun and left uncompleted—of only one.
During his voyage to Naples he often spoke of wishing
to write the story of Sabrina, as indicated in Milton's
"Comus," connecting it with some points in English
history and character.

In prose—apart from his letters, which are noticeably
various in mood, matter, and manner, and contain many
admirable things—Keats wrote extremely little. In a
weekly paper with which Reynolds was connected, *The
Champion*, December 1817, he published two articles
on "Kean as a Shakespearean Actor:" they are not
remarkable. With the above-named articles are now
associated some "Notes on Shakespeare," not written
with a view to publication ; these appear to me somewhat strained and bloated. There are also some "Notes
on Milton's 'Paradise Lost.'" On September 22, 1819,
Keats addressed to Mr. Dilke a letter, which however
does not appear to have been actually sent off. As it
shows a definite intention of writing in prose for regular
publication and for an income, a few sentences are worth
quoting.

"It concerns a resolution I have taken to endeavour

to acquire something by temporary writing in periodical
works. You must agree with me how unwise it is to
keep feeding upon hopes which, depending so much on
the state of temper and imagination, appear gloomy or
bright, near or afar off, just as it happens. . . . You may
say I want tact ; that is easily acquired. . . . I should, a
year or two ago, have spoken my mind on every subject
with the utmost simplicity. I hope I have learned a
little better, and am confident I shall be able to cheat as
well as any literary Jew of the market, and shine up an
article on anything without much knowledge of the
subject—aye, like an orange. I would willingly have
recourse to other means. I cannot; I am fit for nothing
but literature. . . . Notwithstanding my 'aristocratic'
temper, I cannot help being very much pleased with the
present public proceedings. I hope sincerely I shall be
able to put a mite of help to the liberal side of the
question before I die."

On the following day Keats wrote to Brown on the
same subject—

" I will write on the liberal side of the question for
whoever will pay me. I have not known yet what it is to
be diligent. I purpose living in town in a cheap lodging,
and endeavouring, for a beginning, to get the theatricals
of some paper. . . . I shall apply to Hazlitt, who knows
the market as well as any one, for something to bring me
in a few pounds as soon as possible. I shall not suffer
my pride to hinder me. The whisper may go round—I

shall not hear it. If I can get an article in *The Edinburgh*, I will. One must not be delicate."

In pursuance of this plan, Keats did, for a few days in October, take a lodging in Westminster. He then reverted to Hampstead, and finally the scheme came to nothing, principally perhaps because his fatal illness began, and everything had to be given up which was not directly controlled by considerations of health.

CHAPTER VII

H AVING now gone through the narrative of Keats's
life and death, and also the narrative of his
literary work, we have before us the more delicate and
exacting task of forming some judgment of both,—to
estimate his character, and appraise his writings. But
first I pause a brief while for the purpose of relating a
little that took place after his decease, and mentioning
a few particulars regarding his surviving relatives and
friends.

Keats was buried in the Protestant Cemetery at Rome
amid the overgrown ruins of the Honorian walls, sur-
mounted by the pyramid-tomb of Caius Cestius, a
Tribune of the People whose monument has long sur-
vived his fame : this used to be traditionally called the
Tomb of Remus. There were but few graves on the
spot when Keats was laid there. In recent years the
portion of the cemetery where he reposes has been cut off
by a fortification. A little altar-tomb was set up for him,
sculptured with a Greek lyre, and inscribed with his name
and his own epitaph, "Here lies one whose name was
writ in water." Severn attended affectionately to all this,
and the whole was completed about two years after the

poet's death. In 1875 General Sir Vincent Eyre and some other Englishmen and Americans repaired the stone, and placed on an adjacent wall a medallion portrait of Keats, presented by its sculptor, Mr. Warrington Wood. Severn, who died in August 1879, having been British Consul in Rome for many years, now lies in close proximity to his friend. Shelley's remains are interred hard by, but in the new cemetery,—not the old one, which received the bones of Keats. As early as 1836 Severn was able to attest that his connection with the poet had been of benefit to his own professional career. The friend and death-bed companion of Keats had by that time become a personage, apart from the merit, be it greater or less, of his performances as a painter.

Severn's letters addressed to Armitage Brown show that it was expected that Brown should write a Life of Keats. The non-appearance of any such work was made a matter of remonstrance in 1834; and at one time George Keats, though conscious of not being quite the right man for the purpose, thought of supplying the deficiency. Severn also had had a similar idea. Brown was in Italy in 1832, and there he met Mr. Richard Monckton Milnes, afterwards Lord Houghton. He returned to England some three years later, and was about to produce the desired Life when a new project entered his mind, and he emigrated to New Zealand. He then handed over to Mr. Milnes all his collections of Keats's writings, and the biographical notices which he had compiled, and these furnished a substantive basis for Mr. Milnes's work published in 1848—a work written with abundant sympathy,

invaluable at its own date and ever since to all lovers of
the poet's writings.   Brown died towards 1842.

George Keats voluntarily paid all the debts left by his
brother.   These have not been precisely detailed : but it
appears that Messrs. Taylor and Hessey had made an
advance of £150, and there must have been something
not inconsiderable due to Brown, and probably also to
Dilke, who assured George that John Keats had known
nothing of direct want of either money or friends.   George,
who has been described as "the most manly and self-
possessed of men," settled at Louisville, Kentucky, where
he became a prominent citizen, and left a family credit-
ably established.   He died in 1841, and his widow
remarried with a Mr. Jeffrey.   In one of his letters
addressed to his sister, April 1824, there is a pleasant
little critique of "Don Quixote."   It gives one so pre-
possessing an idea of its writer that I am tempted to
extract it :—

" Your face is decidedly not Spanish, but English all
over.   If I fancied you to resemble Don Quixote, I
should fancy a handsome, intelligent, melancholy countenance, with something wild but benevolent about the
eyes, a lofty forehead but not very broad, with finely-
arched eyebrows, denoting candour and generosity.   He
is an immense favourite of mine ; and I cannot help
feeling angry with the great Cervantes for bringing him
into situations where he is the laughing-stock of minds
so inferior to his own.   It is evident he was a great
favourite of the author, and it is evident *he* was united
with the chivalric spirits he so wittily ridicules.   He is

made to speak as much sound sense, elevated morality, and true piety, as any divine who ever wrote. If I were to meet such a man, I should almost hate myself for laughing at his eccentricities."

The opening reference here to a Spanish face must relate to the fact that Miss Fanny Keats, who in girlhood had been the recipient of many affectionate and attentive letters from her brother John, was engaged to, and eventually married, a Spanish gentleman, Senhor Llanos, author of " Don Esteban," " Sandoval the Freemason," and other books illustrating the modern history of his country. He was a Liberal, and in the time of the Spanish Republic represented his Government at the Court of Rome. Mrs. Llanos is still living at a very advanced age. A few years ago a pension on the Civil List was conferred upon her, in national recognition of what is due to the sister of John Keats. There is a pathetic reference to her appearance at the close of the very last letter which he wrote : " My sister, who walks about my imagination like a ghost, she is so like Tom."

Miss Brawne married a Mr. Lindon some years after the death of Keats. I do not know how many years, but it must have been later than June 1825. She died in 1865.

The sincerity or otherwise of Leigh Hunt as a personal, and more especially a literary, friend of Keats, has been a good deal canvassed of late. It has been said that he showed little staunchness in championing the cause of Keats at the time—towards the close of 1818—when detraction was most rampant, and when support from a

man occupying the position of editor of *The Examiner*
would have been most serviceable. But one must not
hurry to assume that Hunt was seriously in the wrong,.
whether we regard the question as one of individual
friendship or of literary policy. The attacks upon Keats-
were in great measure flank-attacks upon Hunt himself..
Keats was abused on the ground that he wrote bad·
poetry through imitating Hunt's bad poetry—that he out-
Heroded Herod, or out-Hunted Hunt. Obviously it
was a delicate task which would have lain before the·
elder poet : for any direct defence of Keats must have·
been conducted on the thesis either that the faults were·
not there (when indeed they *were* there to a large extent) ;.
or else that the faults were in fact beauties, an allegation
which would only have riveted the charge that they were-
Leigh-Huntish mannerisms ; or finally that they were·
not due to Hunt's influence or example, but were proper·
to Keats in person, and this would have been more in
the nature of censure than of vindication. A defence·
on general grounds, upholding the poems without any
discussion of the particular faults alleged, would also, as
coming from Hunt, have been a difficult thing to manage ::
it would rather have inflamed than abated the rancour of·
the enemy. Besides, we must remember that Keats's·
first volume, though very warmly accepted and praised
by Hunt, was really but beginner's work, imperfect in the·
last degree ; while the second volume, " Endymion," was·
viewed by Hunt as a hazardous and immature attempt
notwithstanding its many beauties, and incapable of·
being upheld beyond a certain limit. There was not at
that date any third volume to be put forward in proof of

faculty, or in arrest of judgment. Mr. Forman, than whom no man looks with more patience into the evidence on a question such as this of Hunt's friendship, or is more likely to pronounce a sound judgment upon it, wholly scouts the accusation; and I am quite content to range myself on the same side as Mr. Forman.

Of Keats's friends in general it may be said that the one whom he respected very highly in point of character was Bailey: the one who had a degree of genius fully worthy, whatever its limitations and defects, of communing with his own, was Haydon. Shelley can hardly be reckoned among his friends, though very willing and even earnest to be such, both in life and after death. Keats held visibly aloof from Shelley, more perhaps on the ground of his being a man of some family and position than from any other motive. Shortly after the publication of "The Revolt of Islam," Keats's rather naïve expression was, " Poor Shelley, I think he has his quota of good qualities." Neither did he show any warm or frank admiration of Shelley's poetry. On receiving a copy of " The Cenci," he urged its author to " curb his magnanimity, and be more of an artist, and load every rift of his subject with ore." We should not ascribe this to any mean-spirited jealousy, but to that sense, which grew to a great degree of intensity in Keats, that the art of composition and execution is of paramount importance in poetry, and must supersede all considerations of abstract or proselytizing intention.

CHAPTER VIII.

I MUST next proceed to offer some account of Keats's person, character, and turn of mind.

As I have already said, Keats was a very small man, barely more than five feet in height. He was called "Little Keats" by his surgical fellow-students. Archdeacon Bailey has left a good description of him in brief:—

"There was in the character of his countenance the femineity which Coleridge thought to be the mental constitution of true genius. His hair was beautiful, and, if you placed your hand upon his head, the curls fell round it like a rich plumage. I do not particularly remember the thickness of the upper lip so generally described; but the mouth was too wide, and out of harmony with the rest of his face, which had a peculiar sweetness of expression, with a character of mature thought, and an almost painful sense of suffering."

Leigh Hunt should also be heard :—

"His lower limbs were small in comparison with the upper, but neat and well-turned. His shoulders were very broad for his size. He had a face in which energy and sensibility were remarkably mixed up—an eager power checked and made impatient by ill-health. Every feature was at once strongly cut and delicately alive. If there was any faulty expression, it was in the mouth, which was not without something of a character of pugnacity. His face was rather long than otherwise. The upper lip projected a little over the under; the chin was bold, the cheeks sunken; the eyes mellow and glowing—large, dark, and sensitive. At the recital of a noble action or a beautiful thought, they would suffuse with tears, and his mouth trembled. In this there was ill-health as well as imagination, for he did not like these betrayals of emotion; and he had great personal as well as moral courage. His hair, of a brown colour, was fine, and hung in natural ringlets. The head was a puzzle for the phrenologists, being remarkably small in the skull; a singularity which he had in common with Byron and Shelley, whose hats I could not get on. Keats was sensible of the disproportion above noticed between his upper and lower extremities; and he would look at his hand, which was faded, and swollen in the veins, and say it was the hand of a man of fifty."

Cowden Clarke confirms Hunt in stating that Keats's hair was brown, and he assigns the same colour, or dark hazel, to his eyes : confuting the "auburn" and "blue" of which Mrs. Procter had spoken. It is rather remarkable that, while Hunt speaks of the projection of the *upper* lip—a detail which is fully verified in a charcoal drawing by Severn—Lord Houghton observes upon "the

ꞌundue prominence of the *lower* lip," which point I cannot
trace clearly in any one of the portraits. Keats himself,
in one of his love-letters (August 1819), says, "I do not
think myself a fright." According to Clarke, John Keats
was the only one of the family who resembled the father
in person and feature, while the other three resembled
the mother. George Keats does not wholly coincide in
this, for he says, "My mother resembled John very much
in the face;" at the same time he would not have been
qualified to deny a likeness to the father, of whom he
remembered nothing except that he had dark hair. The
lady who saw Keats's hair and eyes of the wrong colour
saw at any rate his face to some effect, having left it
recorded thus: "His countenance lives in my mind as
one of singular beauty and brightness; it had an expression as if he had been looking on some glorious
sight." In a like spirit, Haydon speaks of Keats as
having "an eye that had an inward look, perfectly
divine, like a Delphian priestess who saw visions." His
voice was deep and grave.

Let us now turn to the portraits, which are as numerous
and as good as could fairly be expected under the circumstances.

The earliest in date, and certainly one of the best from
an art point of view, is a sketch in profile done by
Haydon preparatory to introducing Keats's head into
the picture of Christ's Entry into Jerusalem. The sketch
dates in November 1816, just after Keats had come of
age. The picture is in Philadelphia, and I cannot speak
of the head as it appears there. In the sketch we see
abundant wavy hair; a forehead and nose sloping forward

to the nasal tip in a nearly uniform curve; a dark, set, speaking eye; a mouth tolerably well moulded, the upper lip being fully long enough, and noticeably overhanging the lower lip, upon which the chin—large, full, and rounded—closely impinges. The whole face partakes of the Raphaelesque cast of physiognomy. At some time, which may have been the autumn of 1817, some one, most probably Haydon, took a mask of the face of Keats. In respect of actual form, this is necessarily the final test of what the poet was like—but masks are often only partially true to the *impression* of a face. This mask confirms Haydon's sketch markedly; allowing only for the points that Haydon has rather emphasized the length of the nose, and attenuated (so far as one can judge from a profile) its thickness, and has given very much more of the overhanging of the upper lip—but this last would, by the very conditions of mask-taking, be there reduced to a minimum. On the whole we may say that, after considering reciprocally Haydon's sketch and the mask, we know very adequately what Keats's face was— he had ample reason for acquitting himself of being "a fright." We come still closer to a firm conclusion upon taking into account, along with these two records, two of the portraits left to us by Severn. One is a miniature, which was exhibited at the Royal Academy in 1819, and which we may surmise to have been painted in that year, or late in 1818: the well-known likeness which represents Keats in three-quarters face, looking earnestly forwards, and resting his chin upon his left hand. Here the eyes are larger than in Haydon's sketch, and the upper lip shorter, while the forehead seems straighter; but, as to

those matters of lip and forehead, a profile tells the plainer
tale.   The whole aspect of the face is not greatly unlike
Byron's.   There is also the earlier charcoal drawing by
Severn, the best of all for enabling us to judge of the
beautiful rippling long hair; it is a profile, and extremely
like Haydon's profile, except for the greater straightness
of the forehead, and the decided smallness of the chin,
points on which the mask shows conclusively that
Haydon was in the right.   Most touching of all as a
reminiscence is the Indian-ink drawing which Severn
made of his dying friend on "28 Jan$^{y.}$ 1821, 3 o'clock
morn$^{g.}$," as he lay asleep, with the death-damp on his
dark hair.   It exhibits the attenuation of disease, but
without absolute painfulness, and produces, fully as much
as any of the other portraits, the impression of a fine
and distinguished mould of face.   Severn left yet other
likenesses of Keats—posthumous, and of inferior interest.   There is moreover a chalk drawing by the
painter Hilton, who used to meet Keats at the house
of the publisher Mr. Taylor.   It has an artificial air, and
conveys a notion of the general character of the face
different from the other records, but may assist us
towards estimating what Keats was like about, or very
soon before, the commencement of his fatal illness.
Lastly, though the list of extant portraits is not even
thus exhausted, I mention the medallion by Girometti,
which is to all appearance a posthumous performance.
Its lines correspond pretty well with the profile sketch by
Haydon, while in character it assimilates more to Hilton's
drawing.   To me it seems of very little importance as a
document, but Hamilton Reynolds thought it the best.

likeness of all. Mrs. Llanos was in favour of the mask;
Mr. Cowden Clarke, of the crayon drawing by Severn—
which, indeed, conveys a bright impression of eager,
youthful impulsiveness.

The character of Keats appears to me not a very easy
one to expound. To begin with, it stands to reason that
a man who died at the age of twenty-five can only have
half evolved and evinced himself; there must have been
a great deal which time and trial, had these been granted,
would have developed, but which untimely fate left to con-
jecture. We are thus compelled to judge of an apprentice
in the severe school of life as if he had gone through
its full course ; many things about him may, in their real
nature, have been fleeting and tentative, which to us pass
for final and established. This difficulty has to be allowed
for, but cannot be got over; the only Keats with whom
we have to deal is the Keats who had not completed his
twenty-sixth year. For him, as for other youths, the tree
of the knowledge of good and evil had budded apace;
the fruit remained for ever unmatured. Another gravely
deflecting force in our estimation of the character of Keats
consists in the fact that what we really care for in him is
his poetry. We admire his poetry, and condole his in-
equitable treatment, and his hard and premature fate,
and are disposed to see his life in the light of his verse
and his sufferings. Hence arises a facile and perhaps
vapid enthusiasm, with an inclination to praise through
thick and thin, or to ignore such points as may not be
susceptible of praise. The sympathetic biographer is a
very pleasant fellow ; but the truthful biographer also has
something to say for himself in the long run. I aspire

to the part of the truthful biographer, duly sympathetic.

We have already seen that Keats in early childhood was vehement and ungovernable. His sensibility displayed itself in the strongest contrasts, and he would be convulsed with laughter or with tears, rapidly interchanged. At school his skill in bodily exercises, and his marked generosity of spirit, made him very popular— his comrades surmising that he would turn out superior in some active career, such as soldiering. To be rated as a good boy was not his ambition ; but, as previously stated, he settled down into a very attentive scholar. Later on, his friend Bailey liked " the simplicity of his character," and his winning affectionate manner. " Simplicity " means, I suppose, frankness or straightforwardness ; for I cannot see that Keats's character was at any time particularly simple—I should rather say that it was complex and many-sided.

The one great craving of Keats, before the love for Miss Brawne engrossed him, was the desire to become an excellent poet ; to do great things in poesy, and leave a name among the immortals. At times he was conscious of some presumption in this craving ; but mostly it seems to have held such plenary possession of him that the question of presumption or otherwise hardly arose. Whether he felt very strongly upon any matters of intellectual or general concern other than poetic ones may admit of some doubt. In Book II. of "Endymion" he openly proclaims that poetic love-making is the one thing needful to the susceptible mind ; the Athenian admiral and his auspicious owl, the Indian expeditions

of Alexander, Ulysses and the Cyclops, the death-day of
empires, are as nothing to Juliet's passion, Hero's tears,
Imogen's swoon, and Pastorella in the bandits' den.
He does indeed, in one of his letters (April 1818),
aver "I would jump down Ætna for any great public
good"; but it may perhaps be permissible to think that
he would at all events have postponed the Empedoclean
feat until he had written and ensured the publishing
of some poem upon which he could be content to stake
his claim to permanent poetic renown. His tension of
thought was great. In a letter which he addressed in
May 1817 to Leigh Hunt there is a little passage which
may be worth quoting here, along with Mr. Dilke's comment upon it:

"I went to the Isle of Wight. Thought so much about
poetry so long together that I could not get to sleep at
night; and moreover, I know not how it was, I could
not get wholesome food. By this means, in a week or
so, I became not over-capable in my upper stories, and
set off pell-mell for Margate, at least a hundred and fifty
miles, because forsooth I fancied that I should like my
old lodging here, and could continue to do without trees.
Another thing, I was too much in solitude, and conse-
quently was obliged to be in continual burning of
thought, as an only resource."

This passage Mr. Dilke considered "an exact picture
of the man's mind and character," adding: "He could
at any time have 'thought himself out,' mind and body.
Thought was intense with him, and seemed at times to

assume a reality that influenced his conduct, and, I have
no doubt, helped to wear him out."

Whether Keats should be regarded as a young man
tolerably regular in his mode of life, or manifestly tending to the irregular, is a question not entirely clear. We
have seen something of a sexual misadventure in Oxford,
and of six weeks of hard drinking, attested by Haydon;
and it should be added that two or three of Keats's minor
poems have a certain unmistakable twang of erotic
laxity. Lord Houghton thought that in the winter of
1817–18 the poet had indulged somewhat "in that
dissipation which is the natural outlet for the young
energies of ardent temperaments;" but he held that it
all amounted to no more than "a little too much rollick-
ing" (Keats's own phrase), and he would not allow that
either drinking or gaming had proceeded to any serious
extent, "for, in his letters to his brothers, he speaks of
having drunk too much as a rare piece of joviality, and
of having won £10 at cards as a great hit." Medical
students, it may be added, are not, as a rule, conspicuous
for mortifying the flesh; Keats, however, according to
Mr. Stephens, did not indulge in any vice during his
term of studentship. He was eminently open, as his
writings evidence, to impressions of enjoyment; and one
may not unnaturally suppose that the joys of sense
numbered him, no less than the average of young men,
among their votaries—not indeed among their slaves.
He had not, I think, any taste for those "manly recrea-
tions" which consist chiefly in making the lower animals
uncomfortable, or in putting a quietus to their comforts
and discomforts along with their lives. I only observe

one occasion on which he went out with a gun. He then (towards the close of 1818) accompanied Mr. Dilke in shooting on Hampstead Heath, and his trophy was a solitary tomtit.

As to strength or stability of character, it is rather amusing to find Keats picking a hole in Haydon, while Haydon could probe a joint in the armour of Keats. In November 1817 Haydon had been playing rather fast and loose (so at least it seemed to Keats and to his friend Bailey) with a pictorial aspirant named Cripps, and Keats wrote to Bailey in the following terms :

"To a man of your nature such a letter as Haydon's must have been extremely cutting. . . . As soon as I had known Haydon three days, I had got enough of his character not to have been surprised at such a letter as he has hurt you with. Nor, when I knew it, was it a principle with me to drop his acquaintance, although with you it would have been an imperious feeling. . . . I must say one thing that has pressed upon me lately, and increased my humility and capability of submission, and that is this truth : *Men of genius* are great as certain ethereal chemicals operating on a mass of neutral intellect ; but they *have not any individuality, any determined character.*"

The following also, from a letter of January 1818 to the same correspondent, relates partly to Haydon :

"The sure way, Bailey, is first to know a man's faults, and then be passive. If after that he insensibly draws you towards him, then you have no power to break the link."

Haydon's verdict upon Keats is no doubt extremely important. I give here the whole entry in his diary, 29th of March 1821, omitting only two passages which have been already extracted in their more essential · context :—

"Keats, too, is gone! He died at Rome, the 23rd February, aged twenty-five. A genius more purely poetical never existed. In fireside conversation he was weak and inconsistent, but he was in his glory in the fields. The humming of a bee, the sight of a flower, the glitter of the sun, seemed to make his nature tremble; then his eyes flashed, his cheeks glowed, his mouth quivered. He was the most unselfish of human creatures; unadapted to this world, he cared not for himself, and put himself to any inconvenience for the sake of his friends. He was haughty, and had a fierce hatred of rank [this corresponds with Hunt's remark, that Keats looked upon a man of birth as his natural enemy], but he had a kind, gentle heart, and would have shared his fortune with any man who wanted it. His classical knowledge was inconsiderable, but he could feel the beauties of the classical writers. He had an exquisite sense of humour, and too refined a notion of female purity to bear the little sweet arts of love with patience. *He had no decision of character*, and, having no object upon which to direct his great powers, was at the mercy of every pretty theory Hunt's ingenuity might start.

One day he was full of an epic poem; the next day epic poems were splendid impositions on the world. Never for two days did he know his own intentions. . . . The death of his brother wounded him deeply, and it appeared to me that he began to droop from that hour. I was much attracted to Keats, and he had a fellow-feeling for me. I was angry because he would not bend his great powers to some definite object, and always told him so. Latterly he grew irritated because I would shake my head at his irregularities, and tell him that he would destroy himself. . . . Poor dear Keats! had nature given you firmness as well as fineness of nerve, you would have been glorious in your maturity as great in your promise. May your kind and gentle spirit be now mingling with those of Shakespeare and Milton, before whose minds you have so often bowed! May you be considered worthy of admission to share their musings in heaven, as you were fit to comprehend their imaginations on earth! Dear Keats, hail and adieu for some six or seven years, and I shall meet you. I have enjoyed Shakespeare more with Keats than with any other human creature."

In writing to Miss Mitford, Haydon added:

" His ruin was owing to *his want of decision of character, and power of will,* without which genius is a curse."

It will be seen that Haydon's character of Keats is in some respects very highly laudatory: he speaks of the poet's unselfishness and generosity in terms which may possibly run into excess, but cannot assuredly have fallen short. What he remarks as to "irregularities" seems to show that these had (at least in Haydon's opinion) taken somewhat firm root with Keats, and had not merely come and gone with a spurt, as a relief from feelings of depression or mortification; nor can we altogether forget the statement that, on the night of February 3, 1820, which closed with the first attack of blood-spitting, Keats "returned home in a state of strange physical excitement—it might have appeared to those who did not know him one of fierce intoxication." Physical excitement which looks like fierce intoxication, without being really anything of the sort, can be but a comparatively rare phænomenon; nor do I suppose that an impending attack of blood-spitting would account for such an appearance. Brown, however, was still more positive than Lord Houghton in excluding the idea of intoxication on that occasion; he even says, "Such a state in him, I knew, was impossible"—an assertion which we have to balance against the general averments of Haydon. Keats's irritation at the remonstrances which Haydon addressed to him upon irregularities, real or assumed, is mentioned by the painter without any seeming knowledge of the fact that Keats had (as shown by his letter of September 20, 1819, already cited, to his brother George) cooled down very greatly in his cordiality to his monitor; aud he may perhaps have received the remonstrances in a spirit of stubbornness, or of apparent irritation, more because he was out of humour with Haydon than because he could not confute the allegations, had he been so minded. As to the charge of want of decision of character, want of power of will, we must try to understand what is the exact sense in which Haydon applies these terms. He appears from the context to refer more to indefiniteness of literary aim, combined with sensitiveness to critical detraction and ridicule, than to anything really affecting the basis of a man's character in his general walk of life and commerce with the world. A few words on both these aspects of the question will not be wasted. We need not, however, recur to the allegation of over-sensitiveness to criticism, or of being "snuffed out by an article," which has already been sufficiently debated.

Indefiniteness of literary aim must be assessed in relation to a man's faculties, and in especial to his age and experience. A beginner is naturally indefinite in aim, in the sense that he tries his hand at various things, and only after making several experiments does he learn which things he can manage well, and which less than well. Keats, in his first two volumes, was but a beginner, and a youthful beginner. If they show indefiniteness of aim—though indeed they hardly *do* show that in any marked degree—one cannot regard the fact as derogatory to the author. With his third volume, he was getting some assurance of the direction in which his power lay. It is certainly true that, after producing one epic (if such it can be called), "Endymion," and after commencing another, "Hyperion," he laid the second aside, for whatever reason; partly, it would seem, because the harsh reception of "Endymion" discouraged him, and partly because he considered the turn of diction too obviously

Miltonic; and no doubt, as his mood varied, he must
have expressed to Haydon very divergent opinions as to
the expediency of writing epics.   But, apart from this
special matter, the third volume shows no uncertainty
or infirmity of purpose.   It contains three narrative
poems — "Isabella," "The Eve of St. Agnes," and
"Lamia"—some odes, and a few minor lyrics.   The
very fact that he continued writing poetry so persistently,
maugre *Blackwood's Magazine* and *The Quarterly Review*,
speaks to some decision of character and power of will
in literary matters; and the immense advance in executive force tells the same tale aboundingly.   Therefore,
while laying great stress upon Haydon's view so far as it
concerns certain shifting currents of thought and of talk,
I cannot find that Keats is fairly open to the charge of
want of decision or of will in the literary relation.   Then
as to the larger question of his character generally.
Keats appears to me to have been eminently wilful, and
somewhat wayward to boot.   He had the temperament
of a man of genius, liable to sudden and sharp impressions, and apt to go considerable lengths at the beck of
an impulse, or even of a caprice.   Wilfulness along with
waywardness is certainly not quite the same thing as
"power of will," but it testifies to a will which can exert
itself steadily if it likes.   The very short duration of
Keats's life, and the painful conjuncture of circumstances
which made his last year a despairing struggle between a
passionate love and an inexorable disease, preclude our
forming a very distinct opinion of what his power of will
might naturally have become.   If I may venture a surmise, I would say that he had within him the stuff of

ample determination and high-heartedness in any matters upon which he was in earnest, mingled however with deficient self-control, and with a perilous facility for seeing the seamy side of life.

Lord Houghton gives an attractive picture of Keats at what was probably his happiest time, the winter of 1817–18, when "Endymion" was preparing for the press. I cannot condense it to any purpose, and certainly cannot improve it, so I reproduce the passage as it stands:

"Keats passed the winter of 1817–18 at Hampstead, gaily enough among his friends. His society was much sought after, from the delightful combination of earnestness and pleasantry which distinguished his intercourse with all men. There was no effort about him to say fine things, but he *did* say them most effectively, and they gained considerably by his happy transition of manner. He joked well or ill as it happened, and with a laugh which still echoes sweetly in many ears; but at the mention of oppression or wrong, or at any calumny against those he loved, he rose into grave manliness at once, and seemed like a tall man. His habitual gentleness made his occasional looks of indignation almost terrible. On one occasion, when a gross falsehood respecting the young artist, Severn, was repeated and dwelt upon, he left the room, declaring 'he should be ashamed to sit with men who could utter and believe such things.'"

Severn himself avers that Keats never spoke of any one unless by way of saying something in his favour.

Cowden Clarke's anecdote tells in the same direction, that once, when some local tyranny was being discussed, Keats amused the party by shouting: "Why is there not a human dust-hole into which to tumble such fellows?" His own Carlylean phrase seems to have tickled Keats as well as others, for he repeated it in a field walk with Haydon: "Haydon, what a pity it is there is not a human dust-hole!"

To this may be added a few words from a letter addressed from Teignmouth by Keats to Mr. Taylor in April 1818:—

"I know nothing, I have read nothing: and I mean to follow Solomon's directions, 'Get learning, get understanding.' I find earlier days are gone by; I find that I can have no enjoyment in the world but continual drinking of knowledge. I find there is no worthy pursuit but the idea of doing some good to the world. Some do it with their society, some with their wit, some with their benevolence, some with a sort of power of conferring pleasure and good humour on all they meet—and in a thousand ways, all dutiful to the command of great Nature. There is but one way for me: the road lies through application, study, and thought. I will pursue it; and for that end purpose retiring for some years. I have been hovering for some time between an exquisite sense of the luxurious and a love for philosophy. Were I calculated for the former, I should be glad; but, as I am not, I shall turn all my soul to the latter."

This "exquisite sense of the luxurious" must have

prompted an interjection of Keats in a rather earlier letter to Bailey (November 1817): "Oh for a life of sensations rather than of thoughts!"

One does not usually associate the suspicious character with the unselfish and generous character. Even apart from Haydon's, there is ample evidence to show that Keats was generous, and, in a sense, unselfish; although a man of creative or productive genius, intent upon his own work, and subordinating everything else to it, is seldom unselfish in the fullest ordinary sense of the term. But he was certainly suspicious. Of this temper we have already seen some painful ebullitions in his letters to Fanny Brawne. These might be ascribed mainly to the acute feelings of a lover, the morbid impressions of an invalid. But, in truth, Keats always was and had been suspicious. In a letter to his brothers, dated in January 1818, he refers, in a tone of some soreness, to objections which Hunt had raised against points of treatment in the first Book of "Endymion," adding: "The fact is, he and Shelley are hurt, and perhaps justly, at my not having showed them the affair officiously; and, from several hints I have had, they appear much disposed to dissect and anatomize any trip or slip I may have made." Still earlier, writing to Haydon, he had confessed to "a horrid morbidity of temperament." In a letter of June 1818 to Bailey he says: "You have all your life (I think so) believed everybody: I have suspected everybody." By January 1820 he has got into a condition of decided *ennui*, not far removed from misanthropy, and the company of acquaintances, and even of friends, is a tedium to him. This was a month before the begin-

ning of his fatal illness.   It is true, he was then in love
He writes to Mrs. George Keats :—

"I dislike mankind in general. . . . The worst of men
are those whose self-interests are their passions; the
next, those whose passions are their self-interest.   Upon
the whole, I dislike mankind.   Whatever people on the
other side of the question may advance, they cannot deny
that we are always surprised at hearing of a good action,
and never of a bad one. . . . If you were in England,
I dare say you would be able to pick out more amusement from society than I am able to do.   To me it is as
dull as Louisville is to you.   [Then follow several
remarks on Hunt, Haydon, the Misses Reynolds, and
Dilke.]   'Tis best to remain aloof from people, and like
their good parts, without being eternally troubled with the
dull processes of their everyday lives.   When once a
person has smoked the vapidness of the routine of
society, he must have either some self-interest or the love
of some sort of distinction to keep him in good humour
with it.   All I can say is that, standing at Charing Cross,
and looking east, west, north, and south, I see nothing
but dulness."

"I carry all things to an extreme," he had written to
Bailey in July 1818, "so that when I have any little
vexation it grows in five minutes into a theme fit for
Sophocles.   Then and in that temper if I write to any
friend, I have so little self-possession that I give him
matter for grieving, at the very time perhaps when I am
laughing at a pun."   A phrase which Keats used in a
letter of the 24th of October 1820, addressed to Mrs.

Brawne, may also be, in the main, a true item of self-portraiture : "If ever there was a person born without the faculty of hoping, I am he." Too much weight, however, should not be given to this, as the poet's disease had then brought him far onward towards his grave. Severn does not seem to have regarded such a tendency as innate in Keats, for he wrote, at a far later date, "No mind was ever more exultant in youthful feeling."

Keats's sentiment towards women appears to have been that of a shy youth who was at the same time a critical man. Miss Brawne enslaved him, but did not inspire him with that tender and boundless confidence which the accepted and engaged lover of a virtuous girl natu-rally feels. With one woman, Miss Cox, he seems to have been thoroughly at his ease ; and one can gather from his expressions that this unusual result depended upon a fair counterbalance of claims. While she was self-centred in her beauty and attractiveness, he was self-centred in his intellect and aspirations. There is an early poem of his—the reverse of a good one—which seems worth quoting here. I presume he may have been in his twenty-first year or so when he wrote it :—

" Woman, when I behold thee flippant, vain,
    Inconstant, childish, proud, and full of fancies ;
    Without that modest softening that enhances
The downcast eye, repentant of the pain
That its mild light creates to heal again ;
    E'en then elate my spirit leaps and prances,
    E'en then my soul with exultation dances,
For that to love so long I've dormant lain.

But, when I see thee meek and kind and tender,
Heavens ! how desperately do I adore
Thy winning graces !   To be thy defender
I hotly burn—to be a Calidore,
A very Red-cross Knight, a stout Leander—
Might I be loved by thee like these of yore.

Light feet, dark violet eyes, and parted hair,
Soft dimpled hands, white neck, and creamy breast,
Are things on which the dazzled senses rest
Till the fond fixèd eyes forget they stare.
From such fine pictures, Heavens ! I cannot dare
To turn my admiration, though unpossessed
They be of what is worthy—though not dressed
In lovely modesty and virtues rare.
Yet these I leave as thoughtless as a lark ;
These lures I straight forget—e'en ere I dine
Or thrice my palate moisten.   But, when I mark
Such charms with mild intelligences shine,
My ear is open like a greedy shark
To catch the tunings of a voice divine.

Ah who can e'er forget so fair a being?
Who can forget her half-retiring sweets?
God ! she is like a milk-white lamb that bleats
For man's protection.   Surely the All-seeing,
Who joys to see us with His gifts agreeing,
Will never give him pinions who entreats
Such innocence to ruin—who vilely cheats
A dove-like bosom.   In truth there is no freeing
One's thoughts from such a beauty.   When I hear
A lay that once I saw her hand awake,
Her form seems floating palpable and near.
Had I e'er seen her from an arbour take
A dewy flower, oft would that hand appear,
And o'er my eyes the trembling moisture shake."

From the opening lines of this poem I gather that

Keats, when he wrote it, had never been in love; but that he had a feeling towards pure, sweet-minded, lovely women, which made him, in idea, their champion and votary. Later on, in June 1818, he wrote to Bailey that his love for his brothers had "always stifled the impression that any woman might otherwise have made upon him." And in July of the same year, also to Bailey :— .

"I am certain that our fair friends [*i.e.* the Misses Reynolds] are glad I should come for the mere sake of my coming; but I am certain I bring with me a vexation they are better without. . . . I am certain I have not a right feeling towards women : at this moment I am striving to be just to them, but I cannot. Is it because they fall so far beneath my boyish imagination? When I was a schoolboy I thought a fair woman a pure goddess; my mind was a soft nest in which some one of them slept, though she knew it not. I have no right to expect more than their reality. I thought them ethereal —above men; I find them perhaps equal—great by comparison is very small. Insult may be inflicted in more ways than by word or action. One who is tender of being insulted does not like to *think* an insult against another. I do not like to think insults in a lady's company; I commit a crime with her which absence would not have known. . . . When I am among women I have evil thoughts, malice, spleen; I cannot speak or be silent; I am full of suspicions, and therefore listen to nothing; I am in a hurry to be gone. You must be charitable, and put all this perversity to my being dis-

appointed since my boyhood. . . . After all, I do think
better of womankind than to suppose they care whether
Mister John Keats, five feet high, likes them or not."

In his letter about Miss Cox as "Charmian," written
perhaps just before he knew Miss Brawne, Keats said :
"I hope I shall never marry. . . . The mighty abstract
idea of Beauty in all things I have ' stifles the more
divided and minute domestic happiness.   An amiable
wife and sweet children I contemplate as part of that
Beauty, but I must have a thousand of those beautiful
particles to fill up my heart. . . . These things, combined
with the opinion I have formed of the generality of
women, who appear to me as children to whom I would
rather give a sugar-plum than my time, form a barrier
against matrimony which I rejoice in."

We have seen, in one of Keats's letters to Miss
Brawne, that he shrank from the thought of having their
mutual love made known to any of their friends.   But
he went further than this.   As well after as before he
had fallen in love with Miss Brawne, and had become
engaged to her, he could express a contrary state of
feeling.   Thus, in addressing Mr. Taylor, on August 23,
1819, he says : "I equally dislike the favour of the public
with the love of a woman ; they are both a cloying
treacle to the wings of independence."   And to his
brother George, September 17, 1819 : "Nothing strikes
me so forcibly with a sense of the ridiculous as love.   A
man in love, I do think, cuts the sorriest figure in the
world.   Even when I know a poor fool to be really in
·pain about it, I could burst out laughing in his face ; his

pathetic visage becomes irresistible." The letters to
George, in fact, give no hint of any love for Miss Brawne,
still less of an engagement.

From all these details it would appear that Keats was
by no means an ardent devotee of the feminine type of
character. He thought there was but little congruity
between the Ideal and the Real of womanhood. He
parted company, in this regard, with Shakespeare and
Shelley, and adhered rather to Milton. So it was before
he was in love; and to be in love was not the occasion
of any essential alteration of view. He ascribed to
Fanny Brawne the same volatile appetite for amusement,
the same propensity for flirtation, the same comparative
shallowness of heart-affection, which he imputed to her
sex in general. He loved her passionately : he believed
in her not passionately, nor even intensely. That he
was hard hit by the blind and winged archer was a patent
fact; but he still knew the archer to be blind.

In a room, says Keats's surgical fellow-student, Mr.
Stephens, he was always at the window peering out into
space, and it was customary to call the window-seat
" Keats's place." In his last illness he told Severn that
the intensest of his pleasures had been to watch the
growth of flowers; and, after lying quiet one day, he
whispered, " I feel the daisies [or " the flowers "] growing
over me." In an early stage of his fatal illness,
February 16, 1820, he had written pathetically to James
Rice: "How astonishingly does the chance of leaving
the world impress a sense of its natural beauties upon
us ! Like poor Falstaff, though I do not ' babble,' I
think of green fields; I muse with the greatest affection

on every flower I have known from my infancy—their
shapes and colours are as new to me as if I had just
created them with a superhuman fancy. It is because
they are connected with the most thoughtless and the
happiest moments of our lives. I have seen foreign
flowers in hot-houses, of the most beautiful nature, but
I do not care a straw for them. The simple flowers of
our spring are what I want to see again." Music was
another of his great enjoyments. He would sit for hours.
while Miss Charlotte Reynolds played to him on the
pianoforte; and a wrong note in an orchestra has been
known to rouse his pugnacity, and make him wish to
"go down and smash all the fiddles." Haydn's sym-
phonies were among his prime favourites, and Purcell's.
songs from Shakespeare. "Give me," he wrote from
Winchester to his sister, in August 1819, "books, fruit,.
French wine, and fine weather, and a little music out of
doors, played by somebody I do not know, and I can
pass a summer very quietly." He would also listen long
to Severn's playing, following the air with a low kind of
recitative; and could himself "produce a pleasing
musical effect, though possessing hardly any voice."

Closely though he was mixed up with Leigh Hunt and
his circle, Keats had, in fact, not much sympathy with
their ideas on literary topics, nor with Hunt's own
poetry, still less with their views on political matters of
the time, in which he took but very faint interest.
Cowden Clarke thought that the poet's "whole civil
creed was comprised in the master-principle of universal
liberty, viz., equal and stern justice to all, from the duke
to the dustman. He was, however, a liberal by tem-

perament, and, I suppose, by conviction as well. One of the really puerile and nonsensical passages in "Endymion" is that which opens book iii. He told his friend Richard Woodhouse (a barrister, connected with the firm of Taylor and Hessey) that it expressed his opinion of the Tory Ministry then in office :—

> " There are who lord it o'er their fellow-men
> With most prevailing tinsel ; who unpen
> Their baaing vanities to browse away
> The comfortable green and juicy hay
> From human pastures ; or, oh torturing fact !
> Who through an idiot blink will see unpacked
> Fire-branded foxes to sear up and singe
> Our gold and ripe-eared hopes. With not one tinge
> Of sanctuary splendour, not a sight
> Able to face an owl's, they still are dight
> By the blear-eyed nations in empurpled vests,
> And crowns and turbans. With unladen breasts,
> Save of blown self-applause, they proudly mount
> To their spirit's perch, their being's high account,
> Their tiptop nothings, their dull skies, their thrones,
> Amid the fierce intoxicating tones
> Of trumpets, shoutings, and belaboured drums,
> And sudden cannon."

A rather more sensible embodiment of his political feelings is a stanza which he wrote, perhaps in 1818, at the close of canto 5, book ii. of "The Faery Queen." In this stanza the revolutionary Giant, who had been suppressed by Artegall and Talus, is represented as being pieced together again by Typographus, the Printing-press, and so trained up as to become more than a match for his former victors. There is also, in a letter to

George Keats dated in September 1819, a rather long
and detailed passage on politics covering a wide period
in English and European history, on the oscillations
of governmental and popular power &c., and on the
writer's sympathy with the enlightenment and progress
of the people. It closes with an admiring description
of Sandt, the assassin of Kotzebue, as pourtrayed in a
profile likeness. As to Hunt, some expressions in a
letter from George Keats to Dilke are decidedly strong :
—" I should be extremely sorry that poor John's name
should go down to posterity associated with the little-
nesses of Leigh Hunt—an association of which he was
so impatient in his lifetime. He speaks of him patroni-
zingly ; that he would have defended him against the
reviewers if he had known his nervous irritation at their
abuse of him, and says that on that point only he was
reserved to him. The fact was, he more dreaded Hunt's
defence than their abuse. You know all this as well as
I do."

Apart from his own special capability for poetry, Keats
had a mind both active and capacious. The depth,
pregnancy, and incisiveness, of many of the remarks in
his letters, glancing along a considerable range of subject-
matter, are highly noticeable. If some one were to take
the pains of extracting and classifying them, he would do
a good service to readers. It does not appear, however,
that Keats took much interest in any kind of knowledge
which could not be made applicable or subservient to the
purposes of poetry. Many will remember the ancedote,
proper to Haydon's " immortal dinner " (December
1817), of Keats's joining with Charles Lamb in denounc-

ing Sir Isaac Newton for having destroyed all the poetry
of the rainbow by reducing it to the prismatic colours;
the whole company had to drink " Newton's health, and
confusion to mathematics." This was a freak, yet not so
mere a freak but that the poet—in one of his most
elaborated and heedful compositions, " Lamia "—could.
revert to the same idea—

> "Do not all charms fly
> At the mere touch of cold philosophy?
> There was an awful rainbow once in heaven:
> We know her woof, her texture—she is given
> In the dull catalogue of common things.
> Philosophy will clip an angel's wings,
> Conquer all mysteries by rule and line,
> Empty the haunted air and gnomèd mine,
> Unweave a rainbow."

In a letter to his brother, December 1817, Keats
observes :—

" The excellence of every art is its intensity, capable
of making all disagreeables evaporate from their being
in close relationship with beauty and truth. Examine
' King Lear,' and you will find this exemplified throughout. . . . It struck me what quality went to form a man of
achievement, especially in literature, and which Shakespeare possessed so enormously. I mean *negative capa-*
bility; that is, when a man is capable of being in
uncertainties, mysteries, doubts, without any irritable
reaching after fact and reason. Coleridge, for instance,
would let go by a fine isolated verisimilitude caught from

the penetralium of mystery, from being incapable of remaining content with half-knowledge. This, pursued through volumes, would perhaps take us no further than this : that with a great poet the sense of beauty over-comes every other consideration, or rather obliterates all consideration."

Keats did not very often in his letters remark upon the work of his poetic contemporaries. We have just read a reference to Coleridge. In another letter addressed to Haydon, January 1818, he shows that his admiration of Wordsworth's " Excursion " was great, coupling that poem with Haydon's pictures, and with " Hazlitt's depth of taste," as " three things to rejoice at in this age."

Soon afterwards, February 1818, while "Endymion" was passing through the press, he wrote to Mr. Taylor :—

"In poetry I have a few axioms, and you will see how far I am from their centre. 1st, I think poetry should surprise by a fine excess, and not by singularity ; it should strike the reader as a wording of his own highest thoughts, and appear almost a remembrance. 2nd, Its touches of beauty should never be half-way, thereby making the reader breathless instead of content. The rise, the progress, the setting, of imagery, should, like the sun, come natural to him, shine over him, and set soberly although in magnificence, leaving him in the luxury of twilight. But it is easier to think what poetry should be than to write it. And this leads me to another axiom— That, if poetry comes not as naturally as the leaves to a tree, it had better not come at all."

Keats held that the melody of verse is founded on the adroit management of open and close vowels. He thought that vowels can be as skilfully combined and interchanged as differing notes of music, and that monotony should only be allowed when it subserves some special purpose.

The following, from a letter to Mr. Woodhouse, October 1818 (soon after the abusive reviews had appeared in *Blackwood's Magazine* and *The Quarterly*), is a remarkable piece of self-analysis. As we read it, we should bear in mind what Haydon said of Keats's want of decision of character. I am not indeed clear that Keats has here pourtrayed himself with marked accuracy. It may appear that he ascribes to himself too much of absorption into the object or the personage which he contemplates; whereas it might, with fully as much truth, be advanced that he was wont to assimilate the personage or the object to himself. I greatly doubt whether in Keats's poems we see the object or the personage the clearer because his faculty transpires through them: rather, we see the object or the personage through the haze of Keats. His range was not extremely extensive (whatever it might possibly have become, with a longer lease of life), nor was his personality by any means occulted. But in any event his statement here is of great importance as showing what he thought of the poetic phase of mind and working.

" As to the poetical character itself (I mean that sort of which, if I am anything, I am a member—that sort distinguished from the Wordsworthian or egotistical sublime, which is a thing *per se*, and stands alone), it is not itself—it has no self. It is everything, and nothing—it has no character. It enjoys light, and shade. It lives in gusto, be it foul or fair, high or low, rich or poor, mean or elevated—it has as much delight in conceiving an Iago as an Imogen. What shocks the virtuous philosopher delights the chameleon poet. It does no harm from its relish of the dark side of things, any more than from its taste for the bright one, because they both end in speculation. A poet is the most unpoetical of anything in existence, because he has no identity: he is continually in for, and filling, some other body. The sun, the moon, the sea, and men and women who are creatures of impulse, are poetical, and have about them an unchangeable attribute: the poet has none, no identity. He is certainly the most unpoetical of all God's creatures. If then he has no self, and if I am a poet, where is the wonder that I should say I would write no more? Might I not at that very instant have been cogitating on the characters of Saturn and Ops? It is a wretched thing to confess, but it is a very fact, that not one word I ever utter can be taken for granted as an opinion growing out of my identical nature. How can it when I have *no* nature? When I am in a room with people, if I ever am free from speculating on creations of my own brain, then not myself goes home to myself, but the identity of every one in the room begins to press upon me [so] that I am in a very little time annihilated. Not only among men; it would be the same in a nursery of children." '

Elsewhere Keats says, November 1817: " Nothing.

startles me beyond the moment. The setting sun will always set me to rights ; or if a sparrow come before my window, I take part in its existence, and pick about the gravel."

For painting Keats had a good deal of taste, largely fostered, no doubt, by his intimacy with Haydon. This came to him gradually. Towards the beginning of 1818 he was, according to his own account, quite unable to appreciate Raphael's Cartoons, but afterwards gained an insight into them through contrasting them with some maudlin saints by Guido. It is interesting to find him entering warmly into the beauties of the earlier Italian art, as indicated in a book of prints from some church in Milan (so he says, but perhaps it should rather be Pisa or Florence). "I do not think I ever had a greater treat out of Shakespeare ; full of romance and the most tender feeling ; magnificence of drapery beyond everything I ever saw, not excepting Raphael's, but grotesque to a curious pitch—yet still making up a fine whole, even finer to me than more accomplished works, as there was left so much room for imagination."

Here is a small trait of character, recorded by Keats in a letter to George, from Winchester, September 1819. "I feel I can bear real ills better than imaginary ones. Whenever I find myself growing vapourish, I rouse myself, wash, and put on a clean shirt, brush my hair and clothes, tie my shoe-strings neatly, and in fact adonize as if I were going out ; then, all clean and comfortable, I sit down to write. This I find the greatest relief."

Haydon, as we have seen, said that Keats had an exquisite sense of humour. There are few things more

difficult to analyse than the sense of humour; few points
as to which different people will vary more in opinion
than the possession, by any particular man, of a sense of
humour, or the account, good or bad, to which he turned
this sense.   Certainly there is a large amount of jocularity
in the familiar writings of Keats—often a quick perception of the ridiculous or the risible, sometimes a telling
jest or *jeu d'esprit.* I confess, however, that to myself
most of Keats's fun appears forced or inept, wanting in
fineness of taste and manner, and tending towards the
vulgar; a jangling jingle of word and notion.   Punning
plays a large part in it, as it did in Leigh Hunt's familiar
converse.   Some specimens of Keats's funning or punning seem to me a humiliating exhibition, as, for instance,
a letter, January 1819, which Armitage Brown addressed
to Mr. and Mrs. Dilke, with interpolations by Keats.
No doubt both the friends were resolutely bent upon
being silly on that occasion; but to be silly is not fully
tantamount to being "a fellow of infinite jest," or having
an exquisite sense of humour.   There is some very ex-
asperating writing also in a letter to Reynolds (May
1818), about "making Wordsworth and Colman play at
leap-frog, or keeping one of them down a whole half-
holiday at fly-the-garter," &c., &c.   A feeling for the
inappropriate is perhaps one element of jocoseness; if
so, Keats may have been genuinely jocose when (as he
wrote in his very last letter to Brown) he "at his worst,
even in quarantine [in Naples Harbour], summoned up
more puns, in a sort of desperation, in one week than in
any year of his life."   He had a good power of mimicry,
as well as of dramatic recital.   He did indisputably,

towards September 1819, play off one practical joke—
Brown was the victim—with eminent success; pretend-
ing that a certain Mr. Nathan Benjamin, who was then
renting Brown's house at Hampstead, had written a letter
complaining of illness—gravel, caused by some lime-
tainted water on the premises. But the success depended
upon a very singular coincidence, viz., that by mere
chance Keats had happened to give the tenant's name
correctly. The angry reply of Brown to the angry sup-
posititious letter of Benjamin, and the astonishment of
Benjamin upon receiving Brown's retort, are fertile of
laughter.

Keats does not appear to have ever made any pretence
to defined religious belief of any sort, nor seriously to
have debated the subject, or troubled his mind about it
one way or the other. He was certainly not a Christian.
His early friend, Mr. Felton Mathew, speaks of him as
" of the sceptical and republican school." On Christmas
Eve, 1816, soon after he had come of age, he wrote the
following sonnet—

" The church-bells toll a melancholy round,
    Calling the people to some other prayers,
    Some other gloominess, more dreadful cares,
More hearkening to the sermon's horrid sound.
Surely the mind of man is closely bound
    In some black spell : seeing that each one tears
    Himself from fireside joys and Lydian airs,
And converse high of those with glory crowned.

Still, still they toll : and I should feel a damp,
    A chill as from a tomb, did I not know

> That they are dying like an outburnt lamp,—
> That 'tis their sighing, wailing, ere they go
> Into oblivion,—that fresh flowers will grow,
> And many glories of immortal stamp."

His sonnet on Ben Nevis, 1818, is also an utterance of scepticism—speaking of heaven and hell as misty surmises, and of "the world of thought and mental might" as a realm of nebulosity. A letter to Leigh Hunt, May 1817, contains a phrase arraigning the God of Christians. To the clerical student Bailey, September 1818, he spoke out: "You know my ideas about religion. I do not think myself more in the right than other people, and that nothing in this world is proveable." The latter clause appears to be carelessly elliptical in expression, the real meaning being "I think [not "I do *not* think"] that nothing in this world is proveable." To Fanny Brawne, towards May 1820, he appealed "by the blood of that Christ you believe in." Haydon tells a noticeable ancedote—the only one, I think, which exhibits Keats as an admirer of that anti-imaginative order of intellect of which Voltaire was a prototype—

"He had a tending to religion when first I knew him [autumn of 1816], but Leigh Hunt soon forced it from his mind. Never shall I forget Keats once rising from his chair, and approaching my last picture, Entry into Jerusalem. He went before the portrait of Voltaire, placed his hand on his heart, and, bowing low,

> 'In reverence done, as to the power
> That dwelt within, whose presence had infused
> Into the plant sciential sap derived
> From nectar, drink of gods,'

(as Milton says of Eve after she had eaten the apple),
'That's the being to whom *I* bend,' said he ; alluding to
the bending of the other figures in the picture, and contrasting Voltaire with our Saviour, and his own adoration
with that of the crowd."

Notwithstanding the general vagueness or indifference of his mind in religious matters, Keats seems to
have been at most times a believer in the immortality of
the soul. Following that phrase of his already quoted
(from a letter to Bailey, November 1817) " Oh for a life
of sensations rather than of thoughts ! " he proceeds : " It
is 'a vision in the form of youth,' a shadow of reality to
come. And this consideration has further convinced me
—for it has come as auxiliary to another favourite speculation of mine—that we shall enjoy ourselves hereafter
by having what we call happiness on earth repeated in a
finer tone. And yet such a fate can only befall those
who delight in sensation, rather than hunger, as you do,
after truth. Adam's dream will do here : and seems to
be a conviction that imagination, and its empyreal re-
flexion, is the same as human life, and its spiritual
repetition." This allusion to "Adam's dream" refers
back to a fine phrase which had occurred shortly
before in the same letter—"Imagination may be com-
pared to Adam's dream; he awoke, and found it truth."
In a letter written to George Keats and his wife, shortly
after the death of Tom, comes a very positive assertion—
" I have a firm belief in immortality, and so had Tom."
This firm belief, however, must certainly have faltered
later on ; for, as we have already seen, one of Keats's

letters to Miss Brawne, written in 1820, contains the phrase "I long to believe in immortality." The reader may also refer to the letter to Armitage Brown, September 1820, extracted in a previous page. Of superstitious feeling I observe only one instance in Keats. After Tom's death, a white rabbit appeared in the garden of Mr. Dilke, and was shot by him : Keats would have it that this rabbit was the spirit of Tom, and he persisted in the fancy with not a little earnestness.

Of Keats's fondness for wine—his appreciation of it as a flavour grateful to the palate, and to the abstract sense of enjoyment—there are numerous traces throughout his writings. We all remember the famous lines in his "Ode to a Nightingale"—

> " Oh for a draught of vintage that hath been
> Cooled a long age in the deep-delvèd earth, . . .
> Oh for a beaker full of the warm South ! " &c.—

lines which seem a little forced into their context, and of which the only tangible meaning there is that the luxury and dreamy inspiration of wine-drinking would relieve the poet's mind from the dull and painful realities of life, and assist his imagination into the dim vocal haunts of the nightingale. There is also in "Lamia" a conspicuous passage celebrating "The happy vintage—merry wine, sweet wine." On claret—as to which we have heard the evidence of Haydon—there is a long tirade in a letter addressed to George Keats and his wife in February 1819. I give it in a condensed form :—

"I never drink above three glasses of wine, and never

any spirits and water. . . . How I like claret! When I
can get claret, I must drink it. 'Tis the only palate affair
that I am at all sensual in. . . . It fills one's mouth with
a gushing freshness—then goes down cool and feverless :
then you do not feel it quarrelling with one's liver. . . .
Other wines of a heavy and spirituous nature transform
a man into a Silenus: this makes him a Hermes, and
gives a woman the soul and immortality of an Ariadne.
. . . I said this same claret is the only palate-passion I
have : I forgot game. I must plead guilty to the breast
of a partridge, the back of a hare, the backbone of a
grouse, the wing and side of a pheasant, and a woodcock
passim."

At a rather later date, October 1819, Keats had "left
off animal food, that my brains may never henceforth be
in a greater mist than is theirs by nature." But I presume this form of abstinence did not last long.

I have now gone through the principal points which
appear to me to identify Keats as a man, and to throw
light upon his character and habits. He entered on life
high-spirited, ardent, impulsive, vehement; with plenty
of self-confidence, ballasted with a large capacity (though
he did not always exercise it to a practical result) for
self-criticism; longing to be a poet, and firmly believing
that he could and would be one; resolute to be a man—
unselfish, kindly, and generous. But, though kindly, he
was irritable; though unselfish and generous, wilful and
suspicious. An affront was what he would not bear; and,
when he found himself affronted in a form—that of press
ridicule and detraction—which could not be resented in

person, nor readily retaliated in any way, it is abundantly
probable that the indignity preyed upon his mind and
spirits, and contributed to embitter the days cut short by
disease, the messenger of despair to that passionate love
which had become the single intense interest of his life.
The single intense interest, along with poetry—both of
them hurrying without fruition to the grave. Keats seems
to me to have been naturally a man of complex character,
many-mooded, with a tendency to perverse self-conflict.
The circumstances of his brief career—his poetic ambition, his want of any definite employment, his association
with men of literary occupation or taste whom he only
half approved, the critical venom poured forth against
him, his love thwarted by a mortal malady—all these
things tended to bring out the unruly or morbid, and to
deplete the many fine and solid, elements in his nature.
With the personal character of Keats, as with his
writings, we may perhaps deal most fairly by saying that
his outburst and his reserve of faculty were such that, in
the narrow space allotted to him, youth had not advanced
far enough to disentangle the rich and various material.
But his latest years, which enabled his poetry to find full
and deathless voice, were so loaded with suffering and
perturbation as to leave the character less lucidly and
harmoniously developed than even in the days of adolescence. From "Endymion" to "Lamia" and the "Eve
of St. Mark," we have, in poetry, advanced greatly towards the radiant meridian: in life, from 1818 to 1821,
we have receded to a baffling dusk.

CHAPTER IX.

WE have seen what John Keats did in the shifting scene of the world, and in the high arena of poesy; we have seen what were the qualities of character and of mind which enabled him to bear his part in each. His work as a poet is to us the thing of primary importance: and it remains for us to consider what this poetic work amounts to in essence and in detail. The critic who *is* a critic—and not a *Quarterly* or a *Blackwood* reviewer or lampooner—is well aware of the disproportion between his power of estimation, and the demand which such a genius as that of Keats, and such work as the maturest which he produced, make upon the estimating faculty. But this consideration cannot be allowed to operate beyond a certain point: the estimate has to be given—and given candidly and distinctly, however imperfectly. I shall therefore proceed to express my real opinion of Keats's poems, whether an admiring opinion or otherwise; and shall write without reiterating—what I may nevertheless feel—a sense of the presumption involved in such a process. I shall in the main, as in previous chapters, follow the chronological order of the poems.

As we have seen, Keats began versifying chiefly under
a Spenserean influence; and it has been suggested that
this influence remained puissant for harm as well as for
good up to the close of his poetic career.   I do not see
much force in the suggestion : unless in this limited sense
—that Spenser, like other Elizabethan and Jacobean
poets his successors, allowed himself very considerable
latitude in saying whatever came into his head, relevant
or irrelevant, appropriate or jarring, obvious or far-
fetched, simple or grandiose, according to the mood of
the moment and the swing of composition, and thus the
whole strain presents an aspect more of rich and arbitrary picturesqueness than of ordered suavity.   And
Keats no doubt often did the same : but not in the
choicest productions of his later time, nor perhaps so
much under incitement from Spenser as in pursuance of
that revolt from a factitious and constrained model of
work in which Wordsworth in one direction, Coleridge
in another, and Leigh Hunt in a third, had already come
forward with practice and precept.   Making allowance
for a few early attempts directly referable to Spenser, I
find, even in Keats's first volume, little in which that
influence is paramount.   He seems to have written because his perceptions were quick, his sympathies vivid in
certain directions, and his energies wound up to poetic
endeavour.   The mannerisms of thought, method, and
diction, are much more those of Hunt than of Spenser ;
and it is extremely probable that the soreness against
Hunt which Keats evidenced at a later period was due
to his perceiving that that kindly friend and genial
literary ally had misled him into some poetic trivialities

and absurdities, not less than to anything in himself which could be taken hold of for complaint.

Keats's first volume would present nothing worthy of permanent memory, were it not for his after achievements, and for the single sonnet upon Chapman's Homer. Several of the compositions are veritable rubbish : probably Keats knew at the time that they were not good, and knew soon afterwards that they were deplorably bad. Such are the address "To Some Ladies" who had sent the author a shell; that "On Receiving a Curious Shell and a Copy of Verses [Moore's "Golden Chain"] from the same Ladies;" the "Ode to Apollo" (in which Homer, Virgil, Milton, Shakespeare, Spenser, and Tasso, are commemorated); the "Hymn to Apollo;" the lines "To Hope" (in which there is a patriotic aspiration, mingled with scorn for the gauds of a Court). "Calidore" has a certain boyish ardour, clearly indicated if not well expressed. The verses "I stood tiptoe upon a little hill" are very far from good, and are stuffed with affectations, but do nevertheless show a considerable spice of the real Keats. Some lines have already been quoted from this effusion, about "flowery nests," and "the pillowy silkiness that rests full in the speculation of the stars." It is only by an effort that we can attach any meaning to either of these childish Della-Cruscanisms : the "pillowy silkiness" may perhaps be clouds intermingled with stars, and the "flowery nests" may, by a great wrenching of English, be meant for "flowery nooks"—nests or nooks of flowers. "Sleep and Poetry" contains various fine lines, telling and suggestive images, and luscious descrip-

tive snatches, and is interesting as showing the bent of
the writer's mind, and a sense of his mission begun.
Serious metrical flaws are perceptible in it here and
there, and throughout this first volume of verse—and
indeed in " Endymion " as well.   One metrical weakness
of which he never got rid is the accenting of the preterite
or participial form " ed " (in such words as " resolved,"
&c.), where its sound ekes out with feeble stress the
prosody of a line.   Two songs which have genuine lyric
grace—dated in 1817, but not included in the volume of
" Poems "—are those which begin " Think not of it,
sweet one, so," and " Unfelt, unheard, unseen."   The
volume contains sixteen sonnets, besides the grand one
on " Chapman's Homer."   The best are those which
begin " Keen fitful gusts are whispering here and there,"
and " Happy is England," and the " Grasshopper and
Cricket," which was written in competition with Hunt.
It seems to me that Keats's production has more of
poetry, Hunt's of finish.   The sonnet " On leaving some
friends at an early hour " is characteristic enough.   This
is as much detail as need be given here to the " Poems "
of 1817.   The sonnet on Chapman's Homer revealed a
hand which might easily prove to be a master's.   All
else was prentice-work, with some melody, some richness
and freshness, some independence, much enthusiasm ;
also many solecisms and perversities of diction, imagery,
and method : and not a few pieces were included which
only self-conceit, or torpor of the critical faculty, or the
mis-persuasion of friends, could have allowed to pass
muster.   But Keats chose to publish—to exhibit his
poetic identity at this stage and in this guise ; and of

course we can see, in the light of his after-work, that the experiment was rather a rash forestalling than a positive mistake.

There are a few other sonnets which Keats wrote in 1817, or, in general terms, between the publishing dates of the "Poems" volume and of "Endymion." Those "On a Picture of Leander," and "On the Sea," and the one which begins "After dark vapours have oppressed our plains," rank among the best of his juvenile productions. A general observation, applicable to all the early work, whether printed at the time or unprinted, is that the ideas are constantly *expressed* in an imperfect way. There are perceptions, thoughts, and emotions; but the vehicle of words is, as a rule, huddled and approximate.

"Endymion" now claims our attention. I believe that no better criticism of "Endymion" has ever been written than that which Shelley supplied in a letter dated in September 1819. Certainly no criticism which is equally short is also equally good. I therefore extract it here, and shall have little to say about the poem which is not potentially condensed into Shelley's brief utterance. "I have read Keats's poem," he wrote: "much praise is due to me for having read it, the author's intention appearing to be that no person should possibly get to the end of it. Yet it is full of some of the highest and the finest gleams of poetry; indeed, everything seems to be viewed by the mind of a poet which is described in it. I think if he had printed about fifty pages of fragments from it I should have been led to admire Keats as a poet more than I ought, of which there is now no danger." In July 1820 Shelley wrote to Keats himself on the

subject, furnishing almost the only addendum which
could have been needed to the preceding remarks : " I
have lately read your 'Endymion' again, and even with
a new sense of the treasures of poetry it contains, though
treasures poured forth with indistinct profusion." As
Shelley shared with Gifford the conviction that it is
difficult to read " Endymion " from book 1, line 1, to
book 4, line 1003, and as human nature has not changed
essentially since the time of that pre-eminent poet and
that rather less eminent critic, I daresay that there are
at this day several Keats-enthusiasts who know *in foro
conscientiæ*, though they may not avow in public, that
they have left " Endymion " unread, or only partially
read.   Others have perused it, but have found in it so
much "indistinct profusion " that they also remain after
a while with rather a vague impression of the course of
the story ; although they agree with Gifford, and even
exceed him in the assurance, that "it seems to be mythological, and probably relates to the loves of Diana and
Endymion." As the poem is an extremely important
one in relation to the life-work of Keats, I think it may
not be out of place if I here give a succinct account of
what the narrative really amounts to.   This may be all
the more desirable as Keats has not followed the convenient if prosaic practice of several other epic poets by
prefixing to the several books of his long poem an
"argument" of their respective contents.

Book 1.   On a lawn within a forest upon a slope of
Mount Latmos was held one morning a festival to Pan.
The young huntsman-chieftain Endymion attended, but
his demeanour betrayed a secret preoccupation and

trouble. After the rites were over, his sister Peona addressed him, and gradually won him to open his heart to
her, He told her that at a certain spot by the river, one of
his favourite haunts, he had lately seen a sudden efflor-
escence of dittany and poppies (the flowers sacred to
Diana). He fell asleep there, and had a dream or
vision of entering the gates of heaven, seeing the moon
in transcendent splendour, and then being accosted by a
woman or goddess lovely beyond words, who pressed his·
hand. He seemed to faint, and to be upborne into the
upper regions of the sky, where he gave the beauty a
rapturous kiss, and then they both paused upon a moun-
tain-side. Next he dreamed that he fell asleep. This
was the prelude to his actual waking out of the vision.
Ever since he had retained a mysterious sense that the
dream had not been all a dream. This was confirmed
by various incidents of obscure suggestion, and especially
by his hearing in a cavern the words (we have read them
already, beslavered by the "human serpentry" of criticism, but they remain delicious words none the less)—

> " Endymion, the cave is secreter
> Than the isle of Delos. Echo hence shall stir
> No sighs but sigh-warm kisses, or light noise
> Of thy combing hand, the while it travelling cloys
> And trembles through my labyrinthine hair."

As nothing further, however, had happened, Endymion
promised Peona that he would henceforth cease to live
a life of feverish expectation, and would resume the calm
tenor of his days.

Book 2.—Endymion's promise had not been strictly
fulfilled; he was still restless and craving.   One day he
plucked a rosebud: it suddenly blossomed, and a butterfly emerged from it, with strangely-charactered wings.
He pursued the butterfly, which led him to a fountain by
a cavern, and then disappeared.   A naiad thereupon
addressed him, saying that he must wander far before he
could be reunited to his mystic fair one.   He then
appealed to the moon-goddess for some aid, was rapt
into a dizzy vision as if he were sailing through heaven
in her car, and heard a voice from the cavern bidding
him descend into the entrails of the earth.   He eagerly
obeyed, and passed through a region of twilight dimness
starred with gems, until he reached a natural temple
enshrining a statue of Diana.   An awful sense of solitude
weighed upon him, and he implored the goddess to
restore him to his earthly home.   A profusion of flowers
budded forth before his feet, followed by music as he
resumed his journey.   At last he came to a verdant
space, peopled with slumbering Cupids.   Here in a
beautiful chamber he found Adonis lying tranced on a
couch, attended by other Cupids.[1]   One of them gave
him wine and fruit, and explained to him the winter-
sleep and summer-life of Adonis; and at this moment

----

[1] The passage which begins—

> "Hard by
> Stood serene Cupids watching silently "

has some affinity with a passage in Shelley's " Adonais."   The
latter passage is, however, more directly based upon one in the
Idyll of Bion on Adonis.

Adonis woke up from his trance, and Venus came to solace him with love. Venus spoke soothingly also to Endymion, telling him that she knew of his love for some one of the immortals, but who this was she had failed to fathom. She promised that one day he should be blessed, and with Adonis she then rose heavenward in her car. The earth closed, and Endymion gladly pursued his way through caves, jewels, and water-springs. Cybele passed on her lion-drawn chariot. The diamond path ended in middle air; Endymion invoked Jupiter, an eagle swooped and bore him down through darkness into a mossy jasmine-bower. With a sense of ecstasy, chequered by an unsatisfied longing for his unknown love, Endymion prepared himself to sleep:

> " And, just into the air
> Stretching his indolent arms, he took, O bliss !
> A naked waist. ' Fair Cupid, whence is this ? '
> A well-known voice sighed, ' Sweetest, here am I ! ' "

The lovers indulged their passion in kisses and caresses ; he urgent to know who she might be, and she confessing herself a goddess hitherto awful in loveless chastity, but not naming herself, though perhaps her avowals were sufficiently indicative,[1] and she promised to exalt him ere long to Olympus. The rapturous inter-

---

[1] I do not clearly understand from the poem whether Endymion does or does not know, until the story nears its conclusion, that the goddess who favours him is Diana. He appears at any rate to *guess* as much, either during this present interview or shortly afterwards.

view ended with the sleep of Endymion, and awaking he
found himself alone.　He strayed out, and reached an
enormous grotto.　Two springs of water gushed forth—
the springs of Arethusa and Alpheus, whose loves found
voice in words.　Endymion, sending up a prayer for
their union, stepped forward and found himself beneath
the sea.

Book 3.　Soothed by a moonbeam which greeted him
through the waters, Endymion pursued his course.　Upon
a rock within the sea he encountered an old, old man,
with wand and book.　The ancient man started up as
from a trance, declaring that he should now be young
again and happy.　This was Glaucus, who imparted to
Endymion the story of his ill-omened love for Scylla (it is
told at considerable length, but need not be detailed
here), the witchcraft of Circe which had doomed him to
a ghastly marine life of a thousand years, and how, after
a shipwreck, he came into possession of a book of magic,
which revealed to him that at some far-off day a youth
should make his appearance and break the accursed
spell.　In Endymion, Glaucus recognized the predicted
youth.　Glaucus then led Endymion to an edifice in
which he had preserved the corpse of Scylla, and thou-
sands of other corpses, being those of lovers who had
been shipwrecked during his many cycles of sea-dwelling
doom.　Glaucus tore his scroll into fragments, bound
his cloak round Endymion, and waved his wand nine
times.　He then instructed Endymion to unwind a
tangled thread, read the markings on a shell, break the
wand against a lyre, and strew the fragments of the scroll
upon Glaucus himself, and upon the dead bodies.　As

the final act was performed, Glaucus resumed his youth, and Scylla and the drowned lovers returned to life. The whole joyous company then rushed off, and paid their devotions to Neptune in his palace. Cupid and Venus were also present here; and the goddess of love spoke words of comfort to Endymion, assuring him that his long expectancy would soon find its full reward. She had by this time probed the secret of Diana, but she refrained from naming that deity to Endymion. She invited him and his bride to pass a portion of their honeymoon in Cythera,[1] with Adonis and Cupid. A stupendous festival in Neptune's palace succeeded. Endymion finally sank down in a trance; Nereids conveyed him up to a forest by a lake; and as he floated earthwards he heard in dream words promising that his goddess would soon waft him up into heaven. He awoke in the sylvan scene.

Book 4. The first sound that Endymion heard was a female voice; the wail of a damsel who had followed Bacchus from the banks of the Ganges, and who longed to be at home again, if only to die there. Unseen himself, he saw a beautiful girl, who lay bemoaning her loveless lot. He at once felt that, if he adored his unknown goddess, he loved also his Indian Bacchante. He sprang forward and declared his passion.[2] She, after

---

[1] Keats has been laughed at for ignorance in printing " Visit my Cytherea"; but it appears on good evidence that what he really wrote was " Visit thou my Cythera." A false quantity in this same canto, " Nèptūnus," cannot be explained away.

[2] Declared it in some very odd lines; for instance—

> " Do gently murder half my soul, and I
> Shall feel the other half so utterly ! "

chaunting her long journeyings in the train of Bacchus, explained that, being sick-hearted and weary, she had strayed away in the forest, and was now but the votary of sorrow. Endymion continued to woo her with sweet words and hot; he heard a dismal voice, "Woe to Endymion!" echoing through the forest. Mercury descended and touched the ground with his wand, and two winged horses sprang out of the earth. Endymion seated his Bacchante upon one horse and mounted the other; they flew upward, eagle-high. In the air they passed Sleep, who had heard a report that a mortal was to wed a daughter of Jove, and who desired to hearken to the marriage ditties before he returned to his cave. The influence of Sleep made the winged horses drowse, and also Endymion and the Bacchante. Endymion then dreamed of being in heaven, the mate of gods and goddesses, Diana among them. In dream he sprang towards Diana, and so awoke; but awake he still saw the same vision. Diana was there in heaven; his Bacchante was beside him lying on the horse's pinions. He kissed the Bacchante, and almost in the same breath protested to Diana his unshaken constancy. The Bacchante then awoke. Endymion, dazed in mind with his divided allegiance, urged her to be gone, and the winged horses resumed their flight. They advanced towards the galaxy, the moon peeped out of the sky, the Bacchante faded away in the moonbeams. Her steed dropped down to the earth; while the one which bore Endymion continued mounting upwards, and he again fell into a sort of trance. He heard not the celestial messengers bespeaking guests to Diana's wedding. The winged horse then carried Endymion down to a hill-top. Here once more he found his beautiful Indian, and for her sake forswore all præterhuman passion. She, however, declared to him that a divine terror forbade her to be his. His sister Peona now re-appeared. She rallied him and the Bacchante on their love and melancholy, both equally obvious, and bade him attend at night a festival to Diana, whom the soothsayers had pronounced to be in a mood peculiarly propitious. Endymion announced his resolution to abandon the world, and live an eremitic life : Peona and the fair Indian should both be his sisters. The Indian vowed lifelong chastity, devoted to Diana. Both the women then retired. The day passed over Endymion motionless and mute. At eventide he walked towards the temple : he heeded not the hymning to Diana. Peona, companioned by the Indian damsel, accosted him. He replied, "Sister, I would have command, if it were heaven's will, on our sad fate." The Indian replied that this he should assuredly have ; as she spoke she changed semblance, and stood revealed as Diana herself. She laid upon her own fears and upon fate the blame of past delays, and told Endymion that it had also been fitting that he should be spiritualized out of mortality by some unlooked-for change. As Endymion kneeled and kissed her hands, they both vanished away. The last words of the poem are—

> "Peona went
> Home through the gloomy wood in wonderment : "

words which may perhaps be modelled upon the grave and subdued conclusion of "Paradise Lost."

This is a bald outline of the thread of story which
meanders through that often-skimmed, seldom-read, not
easily readable poem—in snatches alluring, in entirety
disheartening—the " Endymion " of Keats.   It will be
perceived that the poet keeps throughout tolerably close
to his main and professed subject-matter—the loves of
Diana and Endymion, although the episode of Glaucus,
which is brought within the compass of the amorous
quest, is certainly a very long and extraneous one.   As
we have seen, Keats, when well advanced with this poem,
spoke of it as a test of his inventive faculty : and truly it
is such, but I am not sure that his inventive faculty has
come extremely well out of the ordeal.   The best part
which invention could take in such an attempt would be
a vigorous, sane, and adequate conception of the imagin-
able relation between a loving goddess and her human
lover ; her emotion towards him, and his emotion towards
her ; and his ultimate semi-spiritualized and semi-human
mode of existence in the divine conclave ; along with a
chain of incidents—partly of mythologic tradition, partly
the poet's own—which should illustrate these essential
elements of the legend, and take possession of the reader's
mind, for their own sake at the moment, and for the sake
of the main conception as ultimate result.   Of all this we
find little in Keats's poem.   Diana figures as a very willing
woman, passing out of the stage of maidenly coyness.
Endymion talks indeed at times of the exaltation of a
passion transcending the bounds of mortality, but his
conduct and demeanour go little beyond those of an
adventurous lover of the knight-errant sort who, having
taken the first leap in the dark, follows where Fortune

leads him—and assuredly she leads him a very curious dance, where one cannot make out how his human organism, with respirative and digestive processes, continues to exist. Moreover, the last book of the poem spoils all that has preceded, so far as continuity of feeling is concerned ; for here we learn that no sooner does Endymion see a pretty Indian Bacchante than he falls madly in love with her, and casts to the winds every shred and thought of Diana, already his bride or quasi-bride ; she goes out like a cloud-veiled glimpse of moon-light. True, the Bacchante is in fact Diana herself ; but of this Endymion knows nothing at all, and he deliberately —or rather with fatuous precipitancy—gives up the glorious goddess for the sentimental and beguiling wine-bibber. Diana, when she re-assumes her proper person, has not a word of reproach to level at him. This may possibly be true to the nature of a goddess—it is certainly not so to that of a woman ; and it is the only crisis at which she shows herself different from womanhood— shall we say superior to it ?

In another and minor sense there is no lack of invention in this Poetic Romance. So far as I know, there is nothing in Grecian mythology furnishing a nucleus for the incidents of Endymion's descending into the bowels of the earth, passing thence beneath the sea, meeting Glaucus, and restoring to life the myriads of drowned lovers, encountering the Indian Bacchante, and taking with her an aërial voyage upon winged coursers. These incidents—except indeed that of the Bacchante—are passing strange, and could not be worked out in a long narrative poem without a lavish command of fanciful and surprising touches. The tale of the aërial voyage seems abortive; its natural *raison d'être* and needful sequel would appear to be that Diana, having thus launched Endymion along with herself into the heavenly regions, should bear him straight onward to the high court of the gods; but, instead of that, the horses and their riders return to earth, the air has been traversed to no purpose and with no ostensible result, and Endymion is allowed again to forswear Diana for the Bacchante before the consummation is reached. Presumably Morpheus (Sleep) is responsible for this mishap. His untoward presence in the sky sent the Bacchante, as well as Endymion, to sleep for awhile : when they awoke, Diana had to leave the form of the Bacchante, and, in her character of Phœbe, regulate the nascent moon; though a goddess, she could not be in two places at once, and so the winged horses descended *re infectâ*. This is an ingenious point of incident enough ; but it is just one of these points which indicate that the poet's mind moved in a region of scintillating details rather than of large and majestic contours.

Such is in fact the quality of " Endymion " throughout. Everything is done for the sake of variegation and embroidery of the original fabric ; or we might compare it to a richly-shot silk which, at every rustling movement, catches the eye with a change of colour. Constant as they are, the changes soon become fatiguing, and in effect monotonous ; one colour, varied with its natural light and shade, would be more restful to the sight, and would even, in the long run, leave a sense of greater, because more congruous and harmonized, variety. Lus-

cious and luxuriant in intention—for I cannot suppose
that Keats aimed at being exalted or ideal—the poem
becomes mawkish in result: he said so himself, and we
need not hesitate to repeat it. Affectations, conceits,
and puerilities, abound, both in thought and in diction:
however willing to be pleased, the reader is often discon-
certed and provoked. The number of clever things said
cleverly, of rich things richly, and of fine things finely, is
however abundant and superabundant ; and no one who
peruses " Endymion " with a true sense for poetic endowment and handling can fail to see that it is peculiarly the
work of a poet. The versification, though far from faultless, is free, surging, and melodious—one of the devices
which the author most constantly employs with a view to
avoiding jogtrot uniformity being that of beginning a new
sentence with the second line of a couplet. On every
page the poet has enjoyed himself, and on most of them
the reader can joy as well. The lyrical interludes, especially the hymn to Pan, and the chaunt of the Bacchante
(which comprises a sort of verse-transcript of Titian's
" Bacchus and Ariadne "), are singularly wealthy in that
fancy which hovers between description and emotion.
The hymn to Pan was pronounced by Wordsworth, *vivâ
voce*, to be "a pretty piece of paganism "—a comment
which annoyed Keats not a little. Shelley (in his undis-
patched letter to the editor of the *Quarterly Review*)
pointed out, as particularly worthy of attention, the passages—" And then the forest told it in a dream " (book
ii.) ; ." The rosy veils mantling the East " (book iii.); and
" Upon a weeded rock this old man sat " (book iii.) The
last—relating to Glaucus and his pictured cloak—is cer-

tainly remarkable ; the other two, I should say, not more
remarkable than scores of others—as indeed Shelley himself implied.

To sum up, " Endymion" is an essentially poetical
poem, which sins, and greatly or even grossly does it sin,
by youthful indiscipline and by excess.   To deny these
blemishes would be childish—they are there, and must be
not only admitted, but resented.   The faults, like the
beauties, of the poem, are positive—not negative or neutral.
The work was in fact (as Keats has already told us) a
venture of an experimental kind.   At the age of twenty-
one to twenty-two he had a mind full of poetic material ;
he turned out his mind into this poetic romance, conscious that, if some things came right, others would come
wrong.   We are the richer for his rather overweening
experiment ; we are not to ignore its conditions, nor its
partial failure, but we have to thank him none the less.
If " a thing of beauty is a joy for ever," a thing of alloyed
beauty is a joy in its minor degree.

The next long poem of Keats—"Isabella, or the Pot
of Basil "—is a vast advance on " Endymion " in sureness
of hand and moderation of work : it is in all respects the
better poem, and justifies what Keats said (in his letter of
October 9, 1818, quoted in our Chapter v.) of the experience which he was sure to gain by the adventurous plunge
he had made in " Endymion."   Of course it was a less
arduous attempt ; the subject being one of directly human
passion, the story ready-furnished to him by Boccaccio,
and the narrative much briefer.   Except in altering the
locality from Messina to Florence (a change which seems
objectless), Keats has adhered faithfully enough to the

sweet and sad story of Boccaccio; he has however ampli-
fied it much in detail, for the Italian tale is a short one.
" Isabella" has always been a favourite with the readers
of Keats, and deservedly so; it is tender, touching, and
picturesque. Yet I should not place it in the very first
rank of the poet's works—the treatment seems to me at
once more ambitious and less masculine than is needed.
The writer seems too conscious that he has set himself
to narrating something pathetic; he tells the story
ab extra, and enlarges on "the pity of it," instead of
leaving the pity to speak to the heart out of the very circumstances themselves. The brothers may have been
" ledger-men " and " money-bags " (Boccaccio does not
insist upon any such phase of character), and they certainly became criminals, though the Italian author treats
their murder of Lorenzo as if it were a sufficiently obvious
act in vindication of the family honour; but, when Keats
"again asks aloud " why these commercial brothers were
proud, he seems to intrude upon us overmuch the personality of the narrator of a tragic story, and pounds away at
his text like a pulpiteer. This is only one instance of
the flaw which runs through the poem—that it is all told
as with a direct appeal to the reader to be sympathetic—
indignant now, and now compassionate. Leigh Hunt has
pointed out the absurdity of putting into the mouth of
one of the brother "money-bags," just as they are about
to execute their plot for murdering Lorenzo, the lines
(though he praises the pretty conceit in itself)—

> " Come down, we pray thee, ere the hot sun count
> His dewy rosary on the eglantine."

The author's invocation to Melancholy, Music, Echo, Spirits in grief, and Melpomene, to condole the approaching death of Isabella, seems to me a *fadeur* hardly more appropriate than the money-bag's epigram upon the "dewy rosary." But the reader is probably tired of my qualifying clauses for the admiration with which he regards "The Pot of Basil." He thinks it both beautiful and pathetic—and so do I.

"Isabella" is written in the octave stanza; "The Eve of St. Agnes" in the Spenserean. This difference of metre corresponds very closely to the difference of character between the two poems. "Isabella" is a narrative poem of event and passion, in which the incidents are presented so as chiefly to subserve purposes of sentiment; "The Eve of St. Agnes," though it assumes a narrative form, is hardly a narrative, but rather a monody of dreamy richness, a pictured and scenic presentment, which sentiment again permeates and over-rules. I rate it far above "Isabella"—and indeed above all those poems of Keats, not purely lyrical, in which human or quasi-human agents bear their part, except only the ballad "La Belle Dame sans Merci," and the uncompleted "Eve of St. Mark." "Hyperion" stands aloof in lonely majesty; but I think that, in the long run, even "Hyperion" represents the genius of Keats less adequately, and past question less characteristically, than "The Eve of St. Agnes." The story of this fascinating poem is so meagre as to be almost nugatory. There is nothing in it but this—that Keats took hold of the superstition proper to St. Agnes' Eve, the power of a maiden to see her absent lover under certain conditions, and added to it

that a lover, who was clandestinely present in this conjuncture of circumstances, eloped with his mistress.
This extreme tenuity of constructive power in the poem,
coupled with the rambling excursiveness of "Endymion,"
and the futility of "The Cap and Bells," might be held
to indicate that Keats had very little head for framing
a story—and indeed I infer that, if he possessed any
faculty in that direction, it remained undeveloped up
to the day of his death. One of the few subsidiary
incidents introduced into "The Eve of St. Agnes" is
that the lover Porphyro, on emerging from his hiding-
place while his lady is asleep, produces from a cupboard
and marshals to sight a large assortment of appetizing
eatables. Why he did this no critic and no admirer has
yet been able to divine; and the incident is so trivial in
itself, and is made so much of for the purpose of verbal
or metrical embellishment, as to reinforce our persuasion
that Keats's capacity for framing a story out of successive details of a suggestive and self-consistent kind
was decidedly feeble. The power of "The Eve of St.
Agnes" lies in a wholly different direction. It lies in the
delicate transfusion of sight and emotion into sound; in
making pictures out of words, or turning words into
pictures; of giving a visionary beauty to the closest
items of description; of holding all the materials of the
poem in a long-drawn suspense of music and reverie.
"The Eve of St. Agnes" is *par excellence* the poem
of "glamour." It means next to nothing; but means
that little so exquisitely, and in so rapt a mood of musing
or of trance, that it tells as an intellectual no less than a
sensuous restorative. Perhaps no reader has ever risen

from "The Eve of St. Agnes" dissatisfied. After a while he can question the grounds of his satisfaction, and may possibly find them wanting; but he has only to peruse the poem again, and the same spell is upon him.

"The Eve of St. Mark" was begun at much the same date as "The Eve of St. Agnes," rather the earlier of the two. Its relation to other poems by the author is singular. In "Endymion" he had been a prodigal of treasures—some of them genuine, others spurious; in "The Eve of St. Agnes" he was at least opulent, a magnate superior to sumptuary laws; but in "The Eve of St. Mark" he subsides into a delightful simplicity— a simplicity full, certainly, of "favour and prettiness," but chary of ornament. It comes perfectly natural to him, and promises the most charming results. The non-completion of "The Eve of St. Mark" is the greatest grievance of which the admirers of Keats have to complain. I should suppose that, in the first instance, he advisedly postponed the eve of one saint, Mark, to the eve of the other, Agnes; and that he did not afterwards find a convenient opportunity for resuming the uncompleted poem. The superstition connected with St. Mark's vigil is not wholly unlike that pertaining to St. Agnes's. In the former instance (I quote from Dante Rossetti), "it is believed that, if a person placed himself near the church porch when twilight was thickening, he would behold the apparition of those persons in the parish who were to be seized with any severe disease that year go into the church. If they remained there, it signified their death; if they came out again, it portended their recovery; and, the longer or shorter the time they remained in the building, the severer or less dangerous their illness." The same writer, forecasting the probable course of the story,[1] surmised that "the heroine, remorseful after trifling with a sick and now absent lover, might make her way to the minster porch to learn his fate by the spell, and perhaps see his figure enter but not return." If this was really to have been the sequel, we can perceive that the unassuming simplicity of the poem at its commencement would, ere its close, have deepened into a different sort of simplicity—emotional, and even tragic. As it stands, the simplicity of "The Eve of St. Mark" is full-blooded as well as quaint—there is nothing starved or threadbare about it. Diverse though it is from Coleridge's "Christabel," we seem to feel in it something of the like possessing or haunting quality, modified by Keats's own distinctive genius. In this respect, and in perfectness of touch, we link it with "La Belle Dame sans Merci."

"Hyperion" has next to be considered. This was the only poem by Keats which Shelley admired in an extreme degree. He wrote at different dates: "The fragment called 'Hyperion' promises for him that he is destined to become one of the first writers of the age. . . . It is certainly an astonishing piece of writing, and gives me a conception of Keats which I confess I had not before. . . . If the 'Hyperion' be not grand poetry, none has been produced by our contemporaries. . . . The great proportion of this piece is surely in the very highest style of poetry." Byron, who had been particularly virulent against Keats during his lifetime, wrote

[1] See p. 52 as to Miss Brawne.

after his death a much more memorable phrase : " His
fragment of ' Hyperion ' seems actually inspired by the
Titans, and is as sublime as Æschylus." Mr. Swinburne
has written of the poem more at length, and with carefully weighed words :

" The triumph of ' Hyperion ' is as nearly complete as
the failure of ' Endymion.' Yet Keats never gave such
proof of a manly devotion and rational sense of duty to
his art as in his resolution to leave this great poem un-
finished ; not (as we may gather from his correspondence
on the subject) for the pitiful reason assigned by his
publishers, that of discouragement at the reception given
to his former work, but on the solid and reasonable
ground that a Miltonic study had something in its very
scheme and nature too artificial, too studious of a foreign
influence, to be carried on and carried out at such length
as was implied by his original design. Fortified and
purified as it had been on a first revision, when much
introductory allegory and much tentative effusion of
sonorous and superfluous verse had been rigorously
clipped down or pruned away, it could not long have
retained spirit enough to support or inform the shadowy
body of a subject so little charged with tangible significance."

Mr. Swinburne is a critic with whom one may well be
content to go astray, if astray it is. I will therefore
say that I entirely agree with him in this estimate of
" Hyperion," and of the sound discretion which Keats
exercised in giving it up. To deal with the gods of

Olympus is no easy task—it had decidedly overtaxed Keats in "Endymion," though he limited himself to the two goddesses Diana and Venus, and casually the gods Neptune and Mercury; but to deal with the elder gods —Saturn, Ops, Hyperion—and with the Titans, on the scale of a long epic narration, is a task which may well be pronounced unachievable. The Olympian gods would also have had to be introduced: Apollo already appears in the poem, not too promisingly. The elder gods are necessarily mere figure-heads of bulk, might, majesty, and antiquity; to get any character out of them after these "property" attributes have been exhausted to the mind's eye, to "set them going" in act, and doing something apportionable into cantos, and readable by human energies, was not a problem which could be solved by a poet of the nineteenth century. Past question, Keats started grandly, and has left us a monument of Cyclopean architecture in verse almost impeccable— a Stonehenge of reverberance; he has made us feel that his elder gods were profoundly primæval, powers so august and abstract-natured as to have become already obsolete in the days of Zeus and Hades: his Titans, too, were so vast and muscular that no feat would have been difficult to them except that of interesting us. This sufficed for the first book of the poem; in the second book, the enterprise is already revealing itself as an impossible one, for the council at which Oceanus and others speak is reminiscent of the Pandæmonic council in Milton, and clearly very inferior to that. It could not well help resembling the scene in "Paradise Lost," nor yet help being inferior; besides, even were it equal or preferable,

Milton had done the thing first.   The "large utterance
of the early gods," large though it be, tends to monotony.
In book iii., we go off to Mnemosyne and Apollo ; but
of this section little remains, and we close the poem with
a conviction that Keats, if he had succeeded in writing
"a *fragment* as sublime as Æschylus," was both prudent
and fortunate in leaving it a fragment.   To say that
"Hyperion" is after all a semi-artificial utterance of the
grand would be harsh, and ungrateful for so noble an
effort of noble faculty; but to say that, by being pro-
longed, its grandeur must infallibly have partaken more
and more of an artificial infusion, appears to me criticism
entirely sound and safe.

Mr. Woodhouse has informed us : "The poem, if
completed, would have treated of the dethronement of
Hyperion, the former god of the sun, by Apollo ; and in-
cidentally of those of Oceanus by Neptune, of Saturn by
Jupiter, &c., and of the war of the Giants for Saturn's re-
establishment ; with other events of which we have but
very dark hints in the mythological poets of Greece and
Rome.   In fact, the incidents would have been pure
creations of the poet's brain."   Here again Keats would
have been partly forestalled by Milton : the combat of
the Giants with the Olympian gods must have borne a
very appreciable resemblance to the combat of Satan
and his legions with the hosts of heaven.   How far
Keats's "invention" would have sufficed to filling in this
vast canvas may be questioned.   The precedent of
"Endymion," in which he had attempted something of
the same kind, was not wholly encouraging.   The method
and tone would of course ! ave been very different ; in

what remains of "Hyperion," the general current of diction is as severe as in "Endymion" it had been florid.

The other commencement of "Hyperion" (alluded to in my sixth chapter) was a later version, done in November and December 1819; it presents a great deal of poetic or scenic machinery in which the author's personality was copiously introduced. This recast contains impressive things; but the prominence given to the author as spectator or participant of what he pictures forth was fulsome and fatal. Mr. Swinburne is in error (along with most other writers) in supposing this to be the earlier version of the two.

The tragedy of "Otho the Great," written on a peculiar system of collaboration to which I have already referred, succeeded "Hyperion." It is a tragedy on the Elizabethan model, and we find in scene i. a curious instance of Elizabethan contempt of chronology—a reference to "Hungarian petards." The main factors in the plot are a fierce and fervent love-passion of the man, and an unscrupulous ambition of the woman, reddened with crime. Webster may perhaps have been taken by Keats as his chief prototype. To call "Otho the Great" an excellent drama would not be possible; but it can be read without tedium, and contains vigorous passages, and lines and images moulded with a fine poetic ardour. The action would be sufficient for stage-representation at a time when an audience come prepared to like a play if it is good in verse and strong in romantic emotion; under such conditions, while it could not be a great success, it need not nevertheless fall manifestly flat. Under any other conditions, such as those which prevail nowadays, this tragedy would necessarily run no chance at all. In a copy of Keats which belonged to Dante Gabriel Rossetti I find the following note of his, which may bear extracting : " This repulsive yet powerful play is of course in draft only. It is much less to be supposed that it would have been left so imperfect than to be surmised, from its imperfection, how very gradual the maturing of Keats's best work probably may have been. It gives after all, perhaps, the strongest proof of *robustness* that Keats has left ; and as a tragedy is scarcely more deficient than ' Endymion ' as a poem. Both, viewed as wholes, are quite below Keats's three masterpieces ;[1] yet ' Otho,' as well as ' Endymion,' gives proof of his finest powers." Another note from the same hand remarks : " The character and conduct of Albert [the lover of Auranthe murdered to clear the way for her ambition] are the finest point in the play."

Of the later drama, " King Stephen," so little was written that I need not dwell upon it here.

" Lamia " was begun about the same time as " Otho the Great," but finished afterwards. The influence of Dryden, under which it was composed, has told strongly upon its versification, as marked especially in the very free use of alexandrines—generally the third line of a triplet, sometimes even the second line of a couplet. You might search " Endymion " in vain for alexandrines ; and I will

---

[1] I presume the "three masterpieces" are "The Eve of St. Agnes," "Hyperion," and "Lamia"; this leaves out of count the short "Belle Dame sans Merci," and the unfinished "Eve of St. Mark," but certainly not because Dante Rossetti rated those lower than the three others.

admit that their frequency appears to me to give an artificial tone to " Lamia." The view which Keats has
elected to take of his subject is worth considering. The
heroine is a serpent-woman, or a double-natured being who
can change from serpent into woman and *vice versâ*. In
the female form she beguiles a young student of philosophy, Lycius, lives with him in a splendid palace, and
finally celebrates their marriage-feast. The philosopher
Apollonius attends among the guests, perceives her to be
"human serpentry," and, gazing on her with ruthless
fixity, he compels her and all her apparatus of enchant-
ment to vanish. This is the act for which (in lines partly
quoted in these pages) Keats arraigns philosophy, and
its power of stripping things bare of their illusions. No
doubt a poet has a right to treat a legend of this sort
from such point of view as he likes; it is for him, and
not for his reader, to take the bull by the horns. But it
does look rather like taking the bull by the weaker horn
to contend that the philosopher who saves a youthful
disciple from the wiles of a serpent is condemnably
prosaic—a grovelling spirit that denudes life of its poetry.
Conveniently for Keats's theory, Lycius is made to die
forthwith after the vanishing of his Lamia. If we invent
a different finale to the poem, and say that Lycius fell
down on his knees, and thanked Apollonius for saving
him from such pestilent delusions and perilous blandish-
ments, and ever afterwards looked out for the cloven
tongue (if not the cloven hoof) when a pretty woman
made advances to him, we may perhaps come quite as
near to a right construction of so strange a series of
events, and to the true moral of the story. But Keats's

championship was for the enjoying aspects of life; he may be held to have exercised it here rather perversely. "Lamia" is one of his completest and most finished pieces of writing—perhaps in this respect superior to all his other long poems, if we except "Hyperion"; it closes the roll of them with an affluence, even an excess, of sumptuous adornment. "Lamia" leaves on the mental palate a rich flavour, if not an absolutely healthy one.

Passing from the long compositions, we find the cream of Keats's poetry in the ballad of "La Belle Dame sans Merci," and in the five odes—"To Psyche," "To Autumn," "On Melancholy," "To a Nightingale," and "On a Grecian Urn." "La Belle Dame sans Merci" may possibly have been written later than any of the odes, but this point is uncertain. I give it here as marking the highest point of romantic imagination to which Keats attained in dealing with human or quasi-human personages, and also his highest level of simplicity along with completeness of art.

> "Ah what can ail thee, knight-at-arms,[1]
> Alone and palely loitering?
> The sedge is withered from the lake,
> And no birds sing.

> "Ah what can ail thee, knight-at-arms,
> So haggard and so woe-begone?
> The squirrel's granary is full,
> And the harvest's done.

[1] There are some various readings in this poem (as here, "wretched wight"); I adopt the phrases which I prefer.

"I see a lily on thy brow,
  With anguish moist and fever-dew ;
  And on thy cheeks a fading rose
    Fast withereth too."

"I met a lady in the meads,
  Full beautiful, a faery's child ;
  Her hair was long, her foot was light,
    And her eyes were wild.

"I made a garland for her head,
  And bracelets too, and fragrant zone :
  She looked at me as she did love,
    And made sweet moan.

"I set her on my pacing steed,
  And nothing else saw all day long ;
  For sideways would she lean and sing
    A faery's song.

"She found me roots of relish sweet,
  And honey wild, and manna-dew ;
  And sure in language strange she said—
    'I love thee true.'

"She took me to her elfin grot,
  And there she gazed and sighèd deep,
  And there I shut her wild sad eyes—
    So kissed to sleep.

"And there we slumbered on the moss,
  And there I dreamed—ah woe betide !—
  The latest dream I ever dreamed
    On the cold hill-side.

"I saw pale kings and princes too,
  Pale warriors—death-pale were they all ;
  They cried—'La Belle Dame sans Merci
    Hath thee in thrall.'

" I saw their starved lips in the gloam
With horrid warning gapèd wide ;
And I awoke, and found me here
On the cold hill-side.

" And this is why I sojourn here,
Alone and palely loitering ;
Though the sedge is withered from the lake,
And no birds sing."

This is a poem of *impression.* The impression is immediate, final, and permanent; and words would be
more than wasted upon pointing out to the reader that
such and such are the details which have conduced to
impress him.

In the five odes there is naturally some diversity in the
degrees of excellence. I have given their titles above in
the probable (not certain) order of their composition.
Considered intellectually, we might form a kind of
symphony out of them, and arrange it thus—1, "Grecian
Urn"; 2, "Psyche"; 3, "Autumn"; 4, "Melancholy";
5, "Nightingale"; and, if Keats had left us nothing
else, we should have in this symphony an almost complete picture of his poetic mind, only omitting, or
representing deficiently, that more instinctive sort of
enjoyment which partakes of gaiety. Viewing all these
wondrous odes together, the predominant quality which
we trace in them is an extreme susceptibility to delight,
close-linked with afterthought—pleasure with pang—or
that poignant sense of ultimates, a sense delicious and
harrowing, which clasps the joy in sadness, and feasts
upon the very sadness in joy. The emotion throughout
is the emotion of beauty: beauty intensely perceived,

intensely loved, questioned of its secret like the sphinx, imperishable and eternal, yet haunted (as it were) by its own ghost, the mortal throes of the human soul. As no poet had more capacity for enjoyment than Keats, so none exceeded him in the luxury of sorrow. Few also exceeded him in the sense of the one moment irretrievable; but this conception in its fulness belongs to the region of morals yet more than of sensation, and the spirit of Keats was almost an alien in the region of morals. As he himself wrote (March 1818)—

> " Oh never will the prize,
> High reason, and the love of good and ill,
> Be my award ! "

I think it will be well to cull out of these five odes— taken in the symphonic order above noted—the phrases which constitute the strongest chords of emotion and of music.

(1) " Heard melodies are sweet, but those unheard
> Are sweeter; therefore, ye soft pipes, play on;
> Not to the sensual ear, but, more endeared,
> Pipe, to the spirit, ditties of no tone.

> " Human passion far above
> That leaves a heart high-sorrowful and cloyed,
> A burning forehead, and a parching tongue.

> " Beauty is truth, truth beauty,—that is all
> Ye know on earth, and all ye need to know.

(2) " Too late for antique vows,
> Too too late for the fond believing lyre,
> When holy were the haunted forest boughs,
> Holy the air, the water, and the fire.

" Yes, I will be thy priest, and build a fane
 In some untrodden region of my mind,
Where branchèd thoughts new-grown with pleasant pain,
 Instead of pines, shall murmur in the wind.

(3) " Where are the songs of spring—ay, where are they?
 Think not of them : thou hast thy music too,
While barrèd clouds bloom the soft-dying day,
 And touch the stubble-plains with rosy hue.

(4) " But, when the melancholy fit shall fall
  Sudden from heaven like a weeping cloud,
That fosters the droop-headed flowers all,
  And hides the green hill in an April shroud,
Then glut thy sorrow on a morning rose,
 Or on the rainbow of the salt sand-wave.

" She dwells with Beauty—Beauty that must die ;
  And Joy, whose hand is ever at his lips
Bidding adieu ; and aching Pleasure nigh,
  Turning to poison while the bee-mouth sips.
Ay, in the very temple of Delight
 Veiled Melancholy has her sovran shrine.

(5) " That I might drink, and leave the world unseen,
And with thee fade away into the forest dim :
 Fade far away, dissolve, and quite forget
  What thou among the leaves hast never known,
 The weariness, the fever, and the fret,
  Here where men sit and hear each other groan ;
Where palsy shakes a few sad last grey hairs ;
Where youth grows pale and spectre-thin and dies ;
 Where but to think is to be full of sorrow
  And leaden-eyed despairs ;
Where Beauty cannot keep her lustrous eyes,
 Or new Love pine at them beyond to-morrow.

" Darkling I listen: and for many a time
    I have been half in love with easeful Death,—
Called him soft names in many a musèd rhyme
    To take into the air my quiet breath.
Now more than ever seems it rich to die,
To cease upon the midnight with no pain,
While thou art pouring forth thy soul abroad
    In such an ecstasy.

        " The same that oft-times hath
Charmed magic casements opening on the foam
Of perilous seas in faery lands forlorn.
Forlorn ! the very word is like a bell
To toll me back from thee to my sole self.

" Was it a vision or a waking dream ?
    Fled is that music—do I wake or sleep ?"

To one or two of these phrases a few words of comment may be given. That axiom which concludes the
"Ode on a Grecian Urn "—

    " Beauty is truth, truth beauty,—that is all
        Ye know on earth, and all ye need to know,"

is perhaps the most important contribution to thought
which the poetry of Keats contains : it pairs with and
transcends

    " A thing of beauty is a joy for ever."

I am not prepared to say whether Keats was the first
writer to formulate any axiom to this effect,—I should
rather presume not; but at any rate it comes with peculiar
appropriateness in the writings of a poet who might have
varied the dictum of Iago, and said of himself

    " For I am nothing if not beautiful."

In the Ode, the axiom is put forward as the message of
the sculptured Grecian Urn "to man," and is thus pro-
pounded as being of universal application.   It amounts
to saying—"Any beauty which is not truthful (if any
such there be), and any truth which is not beautiful (if
any such there be), are of no practical importance to
mankind in their mundane condition: but in fact there
are none such, for, to the human mind, beauty and truth
are one and the same thing."   To debate this question
on abstract grounds is not in my province: all that I
have to do is to point out that Keats's perception and
thought crystallized into this axiom as the sum and substance of wisdom for man, and that he has bequeathed
it to us to ponder in itself, and to lay to heart as the
secret of his writings. Those other lines, from the "Ode
on Melancholy," where he says of Melancholy—

> " She dwells with Beauty—Beauty that must die;
>   And Joy, whose hand is ever at his lips
>   Bidding adieu "—

appear to me unsurpassable in the whole range of his
poetry—as intense in imagery as supreme in diction and
in music. They pair with the other celebrated verses
from the " Ode to a Nightingale "—

> " Now more then ever seems it rich to die,
>   To cease upon the midnight with no pain ; "

and—

> " Charmed magic casements opening on the foam
>   Of perilous seas in faery lands forlorn."

The phrase *"rich* to die" is of the very essence of

Keats's emotion; and the passage about "magic casements" shows a reach of expression which might almost
be called the Pillars of Hercules of human language.
Far greater things have been said by the greatest minds :
but nothing more perfect in form has been said—nothing
wider in scale and closer in utterance—by any mind of
whatsoever pitch of greatness.

And here we come to one of the most intrinsic
properties of Keats's poetry. He is a master of *imagination in verbal form* : he gifts us with things so finely and
magically said as to convey an imaginative impression.
The imagination may sometimes be in the substance of
the thought, as well as in its wording—as it is in the
passage just quoted : sometimes it resides essentially in
the wording, out of which thought expands in the reader,
who is made

> " To feel for ever its soft fall and swell,
> Awake for ever in a sweet unrest."

From wealth of perception, at first confused or docked
in the expression, he rose into a height of verbal embodiment which has seldom been equalled and seldomer
exceeded. His conception of poetry as an ideal, his
sense of poetry as an art, spurred him on to artistic
achievement; and in the later stages of his work the
character of the Artist is that which marks him most
strongly. As one of his own letters says, he "looks
upon fine phrases like a lover."

According to Mr. Swinburne, " the faultless force and
profound subtlety of this deep and cunning instinct for
the absolute expression of absolute natural beauty is

doubtless the one main distinctive gift or power which denotes him as a poet among all his equals." We may safely accept this verdict of poet upon poet as a true one : yet I should be inclined to demur to such strong adjectives as " faultless " and "absolute." Beautiful as several of them are, I might hesitate to say that even one poem by Keats exhibits this his special characteristic in a faultless degree, or expresses absolutely throughout a natural beauty of absolute quality. To the last, he appears to me to have been somewhat wanting in those faculties of selection and of discipline which we sum up, by a rough-and-ready process, in the word " taste." He had done a great deal in this direction, and would probably, with a few years more of life, have done all that was needed ; but we have to take him as he stands, with those few years denied. Unless perhaps in " La Belle Dame sans Merci," Keats has not, I think, come nearer to perfection than in the " Ode to a Nightingale." It is with some trepidation that I recur to this Ode, for the invidious purpose of testing its claim to be adjudged " faultless," for in so doing I shall certainly lose the sympathy of some readers, and strain the patience of many. The question, however, seems to be a very fair one to raise, and the specimen a strong one to try it by, and so I persevere. The first point of weakness—excess which becomes weak in result—is a surfeit of mythological allusions : Lethe, Dryad (the nightingale is turned into a " light-wingèd Dryad of the trees "—which is as much as to say, a light-winged *Oak*-nymph of the *trees*), Flora, Hippocrene, Bacchus, the Queen-moon (the Queen-moon appears at first sight to be the classical Phœbe,

KEATS. 201

who is here "clustered around by all her starry Fays," spirits proper to a Northern mythology; but possibly Keats thought more of a Faery-queen than of Phœbe). Then comes the passage (already cited in these pages) about the poet's wish for a draught of wine, to help him towards spiritual commune with the nightingale. Some exquisite phrases in this passage have endeared it to all readers of Keats; yet I cannot but regard it as very foreign to the main subject-matter. Surely nobody wants wine as a preparation for enjoying a nightingale's music, whether in a literal or in a fanciful relation. Taken in detail, to call wine "the true, the blushful Hippocrene"—the veritable fount of poetic inspiration— seems both stilted and repulsive, and the phrase "with beaded bubbles winking at the brim" is (though pictu- resque) trivial, in the same way as much of Keats's earlier work. Far worse is the succeeding image, "Not charioted by Bacchus and his pards"—*i.e.*, not under the inspira- tion of wine : the poet will fly to the nightingale, but not in a leopard-drawn chariot. Further on, as if we had not already had enough of wine and its associations, the coming musk-rose is described as "full of dewy wine"— an expression of very dubious appositeness: and the like may be said of "become a sod," in the sense of "become a corpse—earth to earth." The renowned address—

"Thou wast not born for death, immortal bird !
No hungry generations tread thee down,"

seems almost outside the region of criticism. Still, it is a palpaple fact that this address, according to its place in

the context, is a logical solecism. While " Youth grows
pale and spectre-thin and dies," while the poet would
" become a sod " to the requiem sung by the nightingale,
the nightingale itself is pronounced immortal. But this
antithesis cannot stand the test of a moment's reflection.
Man, as a race, is as deathless, as superior to the tramp
of hungry generations, as is the nightingale as a race :
while the nightingale as an individual bird has a life not
less fleeting, still more fleeting, than a man as an
individual. We have now arrived at the last stanza of
the ode.   Here the term " deceiving elf," applied to "the
fancy," sounds rather petty, and in the nature of a make-
rhyme : but this may possibly be a prejudice.

Having thus—in the interest of my reader as a critical appraiser of poetry—burned my fingers a little at the
clear and perennial flame of the "Ode to a Nightingale,"
I shall quit that superb composition, and the whole quin-
tett of odes, and shall proceed to other phases of my
subject.   The " Ode to Indolence," and the fragment of
an "Ode to Maia," need not detain us ; the former, however, is important as indicating a mood of mind—too
vaguely open to the influences of the moment for either
love, ambition, or poesy—to which we may well suppose
that Keats was sufficiently prone.   The few poems which
remain to be mentioned were all printed posthumously.

There are four addresses to Fanny Brawne, dating
perhaps from early till late in 1819 ; two of them are
irregular lyrics, and two sonnets.   The best of the four
is the sonnet, " The day is gone, and all its sweets are
gone," which counts indeed among the better sonnets of
Keats.   Taken collectively, all four supply valuable evi-

dence as to the poet's love affair, confirmatory of what appears in his letters; they exhibit him quelled by the thought of his mistress and her charms, and jealous of her mixing in or enjoying the company of others.

Keats wrote some half-hundred of sonnets altogether, some of them among his very earliest and most trifling performances, others up to his latest period, including the last of all his compositions. Notwithstanding his marked growth in love of form, and his ultimate sur-prising power of expression—both being qualities pecu-liarly germane to this form of verse—his sonnets appear to me to be seldom masterly. A certain freakishness of disposition, and liability to be led astray by some point of detail into side-issues, mar the symmetry and concen-tration of his work. Perhaps the sonnet on "Chapman's Homer," early though it was, remains the best which he produced; it is at any rate pre-eminent in singleness of thought, illustrated by a definite and grand image. It has a true opening and a true climax, and a clear link of inventive association between the thing mentally signified in chief, and the modes of its concrete presentment. In points of this kind Keats is seldom equally happy in his other sonnets; sometimes not happy at all, but distinctly at fault. There is a second Homeric sonnet, "Standing aloof in giant ignorance" (1818), which contains one line which has been very highly praised,

" There is a budding morrow in midnight:"

but, regarded as a whole, it is a weakling in com-parison with the Chapman sonnet. The sonnets, "To

Sleep" ("O soft embalmer of the still midnight"), "Why did I laugh to-night?" and "On a Dream" ("As Hermes once took to his feathers light")—all of them dated in 1819—are remarkable; the third would indeed almost be excellent were it not for the inadmissible laxity of an alexandrine last line. This is the sonnet of which we have already spoken, the dream of Paolo and Francesca. The "Why did I laugh to-night?" is a strange personal utterance, in which the poet (not yet attacked by his mortal illness) exalts death above verse, fame, and beauty, in the same mood of mind as in the lovely passage of the "Ode to a Nightingale"; but the sonnet, considered as an example of its own form of art, is too exclamatory and uncombined.

There are several minor poems by Keats of which— though some of them are extremely dear to his devotees —I have made no mention. Such are "Teignmouth," "Where be you going, you Devon maid?" "Meg Merrilies," "Walking in Scotland," "Staffa," "Lines on the Mermaid Tavern," "Robin Hood," "To Fancy," "To the Poets," "In a drear-nighted December," "Hush, hush, tread softly," four "Faery Songs." Most of these pieces seem to me over-rated. As a rule they have lyrical impulse, along with the brightness or the tenderness which the subject bespeaks; but they are slight in significance and in structure, pleasurable but not memorable work. One enjoys them once and again, and then their office is over; they have not in them that stuff which can be laid to heart, nor that spherical unity and replenishment which can make of a mere snatch of verse an inscription for the adamantine portal of time.

The feeling with which Keats regarded women in real life has been already spoken of. As to the tone of his poems respecting them we have his own evidence. A letter of his to Armitage Brown, dated towards the first days of September 1820, says, in reference to the "Lamia" volume: "One of the causes, I understand from different quarters, of the unpopularity of this new book, is the offence the ladies take at me. On thinking that matter over, I am certain that I have said nothing in a spirit to displease any woman I would care to please; but still there is a tendency to class women in my books with roses and sweetmeats; they never see themselves dominant." The long poems in the volume in question were "Isabella," "The Eve of St. Agnes," "Hyperion," and "Lamia." In "Hyperion" women are of course not dominant; but, as regards the other three poems, they are surely dominant enough in one sense. In "Isabella" the heroine is the sole figure of prime importance—so also in "Lamia"; and in the "Eve of St. Agnes" she counts for much more than Porphyro, though the number of stanzas about her may be fewer. Nevertheless it might be that the women in the three poems, though "dominant," are "classed with roses and sweetmeats." I do not see, however, that this can fairly be said of Madeline in the "Eve of St. Agnes"; she is made a very charming and loveable figure, although she does nothing very particular except to undress without looking behind her, and to elope. Again, Isabella, amenable as she may be to the censure of the severely virtuous, plays a part which takes her very considerably out of affinity to roses and sweetmeats. To Lamia the objection applies clearly enough; but then she is not exactly a woman, and Keats resents so fiercely the far from indefensible line of conduct which Apollonius adopts in relation to her that it seems hard if the ladies owed the poet a grudge. On the whole I incline to think that they must have been misreported; but the statement in Keats's letter remains not the less significant as a symptom of his real underlying feeling about women.

It has often been pointed out that Keats's lovers have a habit of " swooning," and the fact has sometimes been remarked upon as evidencing a certain want of virility in himself. I cannot affect to be, so far, of a different opinion. The incident and the phrase do manifestly tend to the namby-pamby. This may have been more a matter of affected or self-willed diction on his part—and diction of that kind appears constantly in his earlier poems, and not seldom in his later ones—than of actual character chargeable against himself; yet I would not entirely disregard it in the latter relation either. Keats was a very young man, with a limited experience of life. He had to picture to himself how his lovers would be likely to behave under given conditions; and, if he thought they would be likely to swoon, the probability is that he also, under parallel conditions, would have been likely to swoon—or at least supposed he would be likely. Because he thrashed a butcher-boy, or was indignant at backbiting and meanness, we are not to credit him with an unmingled fund of that toughness which distinguishes the English middle class. The English middle-class man is not habitually addicted to writing an " Endymion," an " Eve of St. Agnes," or an " Ode on Melancholy."

Sensuousness has been frequently defined as the paramount bias of Keats's poetic genius. This is, in large measure, unassailably true. He was a man of perception rather than of contemplation or speculation. Perception has to do with perceptible things; perceptible things must be objects of sense, and the mind which dwells on objects of sense must *ipso facto* be a mind of the sensuous order. But the mind which is mainly sensuous by direct action may also work by reflex action, and pass from sensuousness into sentiment. It cannot fairly be denied that Keats's mind continually did this; it had direct action potently, and reflex action amply. He saw so far and so keenly into the sensuous as to be penetrated with the sentiment which, to a healthy and large nature, is its inseparable outcome. We might say that, if the sensuous was his atmosphere, the breathing apparatus with which he respired it was sentiment. In his best work—for instance, in all the great odes—the two things are so intimately combined that the reader can only savour the sensuous nucleus through the sentiment, its medium or vehicle. One of the most compendious and elegant phrases in which the genius of Keats has been defined is that of Leigh Hunt: "He never beheld an oak tree without seeing the Dryad." In immediate meaning Hunt glances here at the mythical sympathy or personifying imagination of the poet; but, if we accept the phrase as applying to the sensuous object-painting, along with its ideal aroma or suggestion in his finest work, we shall still find it full of right significance. We need not dwell upon other less mature performances in which the two things are less closely interfused. Certainly some of his work is merely, and some even crudely, sensuous : but this is work in which the poet was trying his materials and his powers, and rising towards mastery of his real faculty and ultimate function.

While discriminating between what was excellent in Keats, and what was not excellent, or was merely tentative in the direction of final excellence, we must not confuse endowments, or the homage which is due to endowments, of a radically different order. Many readers, and there have been among them several men highly qualified to pronounce, have set Keats beside his great contemporary Shelley, and indeed above him. I cannot do this. To me it seems that the primary gift of Shelley, the spirit in which he exercised it, the objects upon which he exercised it, the detail and the sum of his achievement, the actual produce in appraisable work done, the influence and energy of the work in the future, were all superior to those of Keats, and even superior beyond any reasonable terms of comparison. If Shelley's poems had defects—which they indisputably had—Keats's poems also had defects. After all that can be said in their praise—and this should be said in the most generous or rather grateful and thankful spirit—it seems to me true that not many of Keats's poems are highly admirable; that most of them, amid all their beauty, have an adolescent and frequently a morbid tone, marking want of manful thew and sinew and of mental balance ; that he is not seldom obscure, chiefly through indifference to the thought itself and its necessary means of development ; that he is emotional without substance, and beautiful without control ; and that personalism of a wilful and fitful kind pervades the mass of his handiwork. We have already seen, however, that there is a certain not inconsiderable proportion of his poems to which these exceptions do not apply, or apply only with greatly diminished force ; and, as a last expression of our large and abiding debt to him and to his well-loved memory, we recur to his own words, and say that he has given us many a " thing of beauty," which will remain "a joy for ever." By his early death he was doomed to be the poet of youthfulness ; by being the poet of youthfulness he was privileged to become and to remain enduringly the poet of rapt expectation and passionate delight.

THE END.

INDEX.

BIBLIOGRAPHY.

BY

JOHN P. ANDERSON

(British Museum).

I. WORKS.

The Poetical Works and other Writings of John Keats, now first brought together, including poems and numerous letters not before published. Edited, with notes and appendices, by H. B. Forman. 4 vols. London, 1883, 8vo.

The Letters of John Keats. Edited by J. G. Speed. (The Poems of J. Keats, with the annotations of Lord Houghton, and a memoir by J. G. Speed.) 3 vols. New York, 1883, 8vo.

A number of letters now included in this work were first published in the New York *World* of June 25-6, 1877, and afterwards reprinted in the *Academy*, vol. xii., 1877, pp. 88-40, 65-67.

II. POETICAL WORKS.

The Poetical Works of Coleridge, Shelley, and Keats. In one volume. Paris, 1829, 8vo.
John Keats (including Memoir), i.-vii. and 1-75.

Standard Library. The Poetical Works of J. K. London, 1840, 8vo.
The first *collected* edition of Keats's Works.

The Poetical Works of J. K. London, 1840, 8vo.
With an engraved frontispiece from the portrait in chalk by Hilton. This book, although dated 1840, was not issued until the following year. The frontispiece is dated correctly.

The Poetical Works of J. K. London, 1841, 8vo,

ii BIBLIOGRAPHY.

The Poetical Works of J. K. A new edition. London, 1851, 8vo.

The Poetical Works of J. K. With Memoir by R. M. Milnes [Lord Houghton]. Illustrated by a portrait and 120 designs by George Scharf, Jun. London, 1854, 8vo.
A small number of copies were struck off upon large paper.

The Poetical Works of J. K. With a life [signed J. R. L.—i.e., James Russell Lowell]. Boston [U.S.], 1854, 8vo.

The Poetical Works of J. K. With a Memoir by Richard Monckton Milnes [Lord Houghton]. A new edition. London, 1861, 8vo.
Upon the reverse of the half-title to the "Memoir" is a wood-cut profile of Keats.

The Poetical Works of J. K. Edited, with a critical memoir, by W. M. Rossetti. Illustrated by T. Seccombe. London [1872], 8vo.

The Poetical Works of J. K. Edited, with an introductory memoir and illustrations, by William B. Scott. London [1873], 8vo.

The Poetical Works of J. K. With a memoir by James Russell Lowell. Portrait and 10 illustrations. New York, 1873, 8vo.
The Memoir was afterwards reprinted in "Among my Books," second series, 1876, pp. 303-327.

The Poetical Works of J. K., reprinted from the early editions, with memoir, explanatory notes, etc. (Chandos Classics.) London [1874], 8vo.

The Poetical Works of J. K. Chronologically arranged and edited, with a memoir, by Lord

Houghton. (Aldine Edition.) London, 1876, 8vo.

The Poetical Works of Coleridge and Keats, with a memoir of each. (Riverside Edition.) 4 vols. in 2. New York, 1878, 8vo.

The Poetical Works of J. K. London [1878], 8vo.

The Poetical Works of J. K. Edited, with an introductory memoir, by W. B. Scott. (Excelsior Series.) London [1880], 8vo.

The Poetical Works of J. K. Edited, with a critical memoir, by W. M. Rossetti. [Portrait, fac-simile, and six illustrations by Thomas Seccombe.] (Moxon's Popular Poets.) London [1880], 8vo.
The same as the edition of 1872. The Memoir was reprinted in "Lives of Famous Poets."

The Poetical Works of J. K., reprinted from the original editions, with notes, by F. T. Palgrave. (Golden Treasury Series.) London, 1884, 8vo.

The Poetical Works of J. K. Edited by W. T. Arnold. London, 1884, 8vo.
There was a large paper edition, consisting of fifty copies, numbered and signed.

The Poetical Works of John Keats. Edited by H. B. Forman. London, 1884, 8vo.

The Poetical Works of J. K. With an introductory sketch by John Hogben. (Canterbury Poets.) London, 1885, 8vo.

III. SINGLE WORKS.

Poems, by John Keats. London, 1817, 16mo.
The Museum copy contains a MS. note by F. Locker.

Endymion; a Poetic Romance. By J. K. London, 1818, 8vo.

Endymion. Illustrated by F. Joubert. From paintings by E. J. Poynter. London, 1873, fol.

The Eve of St. Agnes. By J. K. With 20 illustrations by E. H. Wehnert. London, 1856, 8vo.

The Eve of St. Agnes. Illustrated by E. H. Wehnert. London [1875], 8vo.

The Eve of St. Agnes. Illustrated by nineteen etchings by Charles O. Murray. London, 18·0, fol.

The Eve of St. Agnes, and other Poems. Illustrated. Boston [U.S.], 1876, 24mo.

Miscellanies of the Philobiblon Society. London, 1856-7, 8vo.
    Vol. iii. contains "Another version of Keats's *Hyperion, a Vision*," edited, with an introduction, by R. M. Milnes (Lord Houghton).

Keatsii Hyperionis. Libri i-ii. Latine reddidit Carolus Merivale. Cambridge, 1862, 8vo.

Keats's Hyperion. Book I. With notes [life and introduction]. London [1877], 8vo.

Keats's Hyperion. Book I. With introduction, elucidatory notes, and an appendix of exercises. London [1878], 8vo.

Lamia, Isabella, The Eve of St. Agnes, and other Poems. By J. K. London, 1820, 12mo.

Lamia. With illustrative designs by W. H. Low. Philadelphia, 1885, fol.

Ode to a Nightingale. By J. K. Edited, with an introduction, by Thomas J. Wise. London, 1884, 8vo.
    Printed for private distribution, and issued in parchment wrappers. Four copies on vellum and twenty-five on paper only printed,

IV. LETTERS, ETC.

Life, Letters, and Literary Remains of J. K. Edited by R. M. Milnes. 2 vols. London, 1848, 16mo.

Life and Letters of John Keats. A new and completely revised edition. Edited by Lord Houghton. London, 1867, 8vo.

Letters of J. K. to Fanny Brawne, written in the years 1819 and 1820, and now given from the original manuscripts, with introduction and notes, by Harry Buxton Forman. London, 1878, 8vo.
    In addition to the ordinary issue, the following special copies were "printed for private distribution"— In 8vo on Whatman's hand-made paper 50 copies, on vellum 2 copies; in post 8vo there were 6 copies with title-page set up in different style, and 2 copies of coloured bank-note paper, one blue and the other yellow.

V. MISCELLANEOUS.

CONTRIBUTIONS TO MAGAZINES.

Annals of the Fine Arts. A quarterly magazine, edited by James Elmes—
    "Ode to the Nightingale," vol. iv., 1820, pp. 354-356. The first appearance of this poem, which was afterwards included in the "Lamia" volume, 1820, pp. 107-112.
    "Ode on a Grecian Urn." Appeared first in the "Annals of the Fine Arts" vol. iv., 1820, pp. 638, 639, afterwards included in the Lamia volume.

The Athenæum—
    First appearance of the Sonnet "On hearing the Bag-pipe and seeing 'The Stranger' played at Inverary," June 7, 1873, p. 725.

The Champion—

"On Edmund Kean as a Shakesperian actor, and on Kean in 'Richard, Duke of York.'" Appeared on the 21st and 28th Dec. 1817.

The Dial—

"Notes on Milton's Paradise Lost." In vol. iii., 1843, pp, 500-504; reprinted by Lord Houghton.

The Examiner—

The "Sonnet to Solitude," Keats's first published poem, according to Charles Cowden Clarke, appeared on the 5th of May 1816, signed J. K., p. 282.

The first appearance of the sonnet "To Kosciusko," Feb. 16, 1817, p. 107.

The first appearance of the sonnet, "After dark vapors have oppress'd our plains," etc., Feb. 23, 1817, p. 124.

Two sonnets "To Haydon, with a Sonnet written on seeing the Elgin Marbles," and "On seeing the Elgin Marbles" appear for the first time, March 9, 1817, p. 155. In 1818 they were reprinted in the *Annals of the Fine Arts*, No. 8.

The first appearance of the sonnet, "Written on a blank space at the end of Chaucer's tale of 'The Floure and the Lefe,'" March 16, 1817, p. 173.

Sonnet "On the Grasshopper and Cricket" appeared on the 21st Sept. 1817, p. 599.

The Gem, a Literary Annual. Edited by Thomas Hood—

The sonnet "On a picture of Leander" appeared for the first time in 1829, p. 108.

Hood's Comic Annual—

"Sonnet to a Cat," 1830, p. 14.

Hood's Magazine—

In vol. ii., 1844, p. 240, the sonnet "Life's sea hath been five times at its slow ebb" appears for the first time; included by Lord Houghton in the Literary Remains.

In vol. ii., 1844, p. 562, the poem "Old Meg," written during a tour in Scotland, appears for the first time.

The Indicator. Edited by Leigh Hunt—

In vol. i., 1820, p. 120, there are thirty-four lines, headed *Vox et præterea nihil*, supposed by Mr. Forman to be a cancelled passage of Endymion, and reprinted by him in his edition of Keats, 1883, vol. i., p. 221.

In vol. i. 1820, pp. 246-248, the poem "La Belle Dame Sans Merci" first appeared, and signed "Caviare."

First appearance of the sonnet, "A Dream after reading Dante's Episode of 'Paolo and Francesca,'" signed "Caviare," vol. i. 1820, p. 304.

Leigh Hunt's Literary Pocket Book—

First appearance of the sonnets, "To Ailsa Rock" and "The Human Season" in 1819.

VI. APPENDIX.

BIOGRAPHY, CRITICISM, ETC.

Armstrong, Edmund J.—Essays and Sketches of Edmund J. Armstrong. London, 1877, 8vo.

Keats, pp. 176-179.

Atlantic Monthly.—Boston, 1858, 8vo.

"The Poet Keats." Seven stanzas, vol. ii., pp. 531-532.

Belfast, Earl of. — Poets and Poetry of the xixth century. A course of lectures. London, 1852, 8vo.

Moore, Keats, Scott, pp. 59-131.

Best Bits.—Best Bits. London, 1884, 8vo.

"The Last Moments of Keats," vol. ii., p. 119.

Biographical Magazine.—Lives of the Illustrious (The Biographical Magazine). London, 1853, 8vo.

John Keats, vol. iii., pp. 260-271.

Caine, T. Hall. Recollections of Dante Gabriel Rossetti. London, 1882, 8vo.

Keats, pp. 167-183.

Caine, T. Hall.—Cobwebs of Criticism, etc. London, 1883, 8vo.
Keats, pp. 158-190.

Carr, J. Comyns.—Essays on Art. London, 1879, 8vo.
The artistic spirit in Modern English Poetry, pp. 3-34.

Clarke, Charles Cowden. — The Riches of Chaucer, in which his impurities have been expunged, etc. 2 vols. London, 1835, 12mo.
John Keats, vol. 1., pp. 52, 53.

——Recollections of Writers. London, 1878, 8vo.
John Keats, pp. 120-157.

Colvin, Sidney.—Keats (*English Men of Letters*). London, 1887, 8vo.

Cotterill, H. B.—An Introduction to the Study of Poetry. London, 1882, 8vo.
Keats, pp. 242-268.

Courthope, William J. — The Liberal Movement in English Literature. London, 1885, 8vo.
Poetry, Music, and Painting. Coleridge and Keats, pp. 159-194.

Cunningham, Allan.—Biographical and Critical History of the British Literature of the last fifty years. [Reprinted from the "Athenæum."] Paris, 1834, 12mo.
Keats, pp. 102-104.

Dennis, John.—Heroes of Literature. English Poets. London, 1883, 8vo.
Keats, pp. 365-373.

De Quincey, Thomas. — Essays on the Poets, and other English Writers. Boston, 1853, 8vo.
John Keats, pp. 75-97.

——De Quincey's Works. 16 vols. Edinburgh, 1862-71, 12mo.
John Keats, vol. v, pp.. 269-288.

Devey, J.—A comparative estimate of Modern English Poetry. London, 1873, 8vo.
Alexandrine Poets. Keats, pp. 263-274.

Dilke, Charles Wentworth.—The Papers of a Critic. Selected from the writings of the late Charles W. Dilke. 2 vols. London, 1875, 8vo.
John Keats, vol. 1., pp. 2-14.

Encyclopædia Britannica. — Encyclopædia Britannica. Eighth edition. Edinburgh, 1857, 4to.
John Keats, vol. xiii., pp. 55-57.

——Ninth edition. Edinburgh, 1882, 4to.
John Keats, by Algernon C. Swinburne, vol. xiv., pp. 22-24.

English Writers.—Essays on English Writers. By the author of "The Gentle Life." London, 1869, 8vo.
Shelley, Keats, etc., pp. 338-349.

Gilfillan, George.—A Gallery of Literary Portraits. Edinburgh, 1845, 8vo.
John Keats, pp. 372-385.

Gossip.— The Gossip. London, 1821, 8vo.
Three Stanzas, signed G. V. D., May 19, 1821, p. 96, "On Reading Lamia and other poems, by John Keats."

Griswold, Rufus W.—The Poets and Poetry of England in the Nineteenth Century. New York, 1875, 8vo.
John Keats, with portrait, pp. 301-311.

Haydon, Benjamin Robert.—Life of B. R. Haydon. Edited and compiled by Tom Taylor. 3 vols. London, 1853, 8vo.
Numerous references to Keats.

——Correspondence and Table-Talk. With a memoir by his son, F. W. Haydon. 2 vols. London, 1876, 8vo.
Contains ten letters and two extracts from letters to Haydon, and

ten letters from Haydon to Keats, vol. ii., pp. 1-17.

Hinde, F.—Essays and Poems. Liverpool, 1864, 8vo.
The life and works of the poet Keats: a paper read before the Liverpool Philomathic Society, April 15, 1862, pp. 57-95.

Hoffmann, Frederick A.—Poetry, its origin, nature, and history, etc. London, 1884, 8vo.
Keats, vol. i., pp. 483-491.

Howitt, William. — Homes and Haunts of the most eminent British Poets. Third edition. London, 1857, 8vo.
John Keats, pp. 292-300.

——The Northern Heights of London, etc. London, 1869, 8vo.
Keats, pp. 95-103.

Hunt, Leigh.—Imagination and Fancy; or, selections from the English Poets. London, 1844, 12mo.
Keats, born 1796, died 1821, pp. 312-345.

——Foliage, or Poems original and translated. London, 1818, 8vo.
Contains four sonnets; "To John Keats," "On receiving a Crown of Ivy from the same," "On the same," "To the Grasshopper and the Cricket."

——Lord Byron and some of his Contemporaries; with recollections of the author's life, and of his visit to Italy. London, 1828, 4to.
John Keats, pp. 246-268.

——The Autobiography of Leigh Hunt; with reminiscences of friends and contemporaries. In three volumes. London, 1850, 8vo.
The references to John Keats, vol. ii., pp. 201-216, etc. are substantially reproduced from the preceding work.

Hutton, Laurence. — Literary

Landmarks of London. London, [1885], 8vo.
John Keats, pp. 177-182.

Jeffrey, Francis. — Contributions to the Edinburgh Review. London, 1853, 8vo.
John Keats. Review of Endymion and Lamia, pp. 520-534.

Lester, John W. — Criticisms. Third edition. London, 1853, 8vo.
John Keats, pp. 343-349.

Lowell, James Russell.—Among my Books. Second series. London, 1876, 8vo.
Keats, pp. 303-327.

——The Poetical Works of J. R. L. New revised edition. Boston [U.S.], 1882, 8vo.
Sonnet "To the Spirit of Keats," p. 20.

Maginn, William.—Miscellanies: prose and verse. Edited by R. W. Montagu. 2 vols. London, 1885, 8vo.
Remarks on Shelley's Adonais, vol. ii., pp. 300-311.

Mario, Jessie White.—Sepolcri Inglesi in Roma. (Estratto dalla *Nuova Antologia*, 15 Maggio, 1879.) Roma, 1879, 8vo.
On Keats and Shelley.

Mason, Edward T. — Personal Traits of British Authors. New York, 1885, 8vo.
John Keats, pp. 195-207.

Masson, David. — Wordsworth, Shelley, Keats, and other Essays. London, 1874, 8vo.
"The Life and Poetry of Keats," pp. 143-191.

Medwin, Thomas.—Journal of the Conversations of Lord Byron: noted during a residence with his Lordship at Pisa, in the

years 1821 and 1822. By T. Medwin. London, 1824, 4to.
John Keats, pp. 143, 237-240, 255, etc.

Milnes, Richard Monckton, *Lord Houghton.*—Life, Letters, and Literary Remains of John Keats. In two volumes. London, 1848, 8vo.

——Life and Letters of John Keats. A new and completely revised edition. Edited by Lord Houghton, London, 1867, 8vo.

Mitford, Mary Russell.—Recollections of a Literary Life, etc. 3 vols. London, 1852, 8vo.
Shelley and Keats, vol. ii., pp. 183-192.

Moir, D. M. — Sketches of the poetical literature of the past half-century. London, 1851, 8vo.
John Keats, pp. 215-221.

Noel, Hon. Roden. — Essays on poetry and poets. London, 1886, 8vo.
Keats, pp. 150-171.

Notes and Queries. — General Index to Notes and Queries. 5 series. London, 1856-80, 4to.
Numerous references to John Keats.

Olio.—The Olio. London [1828], 8vo.
" Recollections of Books and their Authors," No. 6, "John Keats, the Poet," vol. i., pp. 391-394.

Oliphant, Mrs. — The Literary History of England, etc. 3 vols. London, 1885, 8vo.
John Keats, vol. iii., pp. 133-155.

Owen, Frances Mary.—John Keats. A Study. London, 1880, 8vo.
Reviewed in the *Academy*, July 5, 1884, p. 2.

Payn, James. — Stories from Boccaccio, and other Poems. London, 1852, 8vo.
Sonnet to John Keats, p. 97.

Phillips, Samuel.—Essays from " The Times." Being a selection from the literary papers which have appeared in that journal. London, 1851, 8vo.
"The Life of John Keats," pp. 255-269. This article originally appeared in " The Times " on Sept. 17, 1849.

——New Edition. 2 vols. London, 1871, 8vo.
John Keats, vol. i., pp. 255-269.

Richardson, David Lester. — Literary Chit-Chat, etc. Calcutta, 1848, 8vo.
Shelley, Keats, and Coleridge, pp. 271-281.

Rossetti, Dante Gabriel.—Ballads and Sonnets. London, 1881, 8vo.
Sonnets "To Five English Poets." No. iv., John Keats, p. 316.

Rossetti, William Michael.—Lives of Famous Poets. London [1885], 8vo.
John Keats, pp. 349-361.

Sarrazin, Gabriel. — Poètes Modernes de l'Angleterre. Paris, 1885, 8vo.
John Keats, pp. 131-152.

Scott, William Bell. — Poems, Ballads, Studies from Nature, Sonnets, etc. Illustrated by seventeen etchings by the author and L. Alma Tadema. London, 1875, 8vo.
An etching by the author of Keats' Grave, p. 177 ; sonnet "On the Inscription, Keats' Tombstone," p. 179. An Ode "To the memory of John Keats," pp. 226-230.

Scribner's Monthly Magazine.— Scribner's Monthly Magazine. New York, 1880, 1887, 8vo.
The No. for June 1880 contains fourteen lines "To the Immortal memory of Keats," and the May No. for 1887, p. 110, " Keats " (ten verses) by Robert Burns Wilson.

Shelley, Percy Bysshe.—Adonais. An elegy on the death of John

Keats, author of Endymion, Hyperion, etc. Pisa, 1821, 4to.

——Adonais. An elegy on the death of John Keats, etc. Cambridge, 1829, 8vo.

——Adonais. Edited, with notes, by H. Buxton Forman. London, 1880, 8vo.

Shelley, Lady. — Shelley Memorials ; from authentic sources. Edited by Lady Shelley. London, 1859, 8vo.
John Keats, pp. 74, 150-152, 155, 156, 200, 203.

Stedman, Edmund Clarence.— Victorian Poets. London, 1876, 8vo.
John Keats, pp. 18, 104, 105, 155, 367, etc.

Swinburne, Algernon . Charles.— Miscellanies. London, 1886, 8vo.
Keats, pp. 210-218. Originally appeared in the Encyclopædia Britannica.

Tuckerman, Henry T.— Characteristics of Literature, illustrated by the genius of distinguished men. Philadelphia, 1849, 8vo.
Final Memorials of Lamb and Keats, pp. 256-269.

——Thoughts on the Poets. London [1852], 12mo.
Keats, pp. 212-226.

Verdicts. — Verdicts. [Verse.] London, 1852, 8vo.
John Keats, occupies 93 lines, pp. 28-32.

Ward, Thomas H.—The English Poets, etc. 4 vols. London, 1883, 8vo.
John Keats, by Matthew Arnold, vol. iv., pp. 427-464.

Willis, N. P.—Pencillings by the Way. A new edition. London, 1844, 8vo.
"Keats's Poems," pp. 84-88.

Wiseman, Cardinal.—On the Perception of Natural Beauty by the Ancients and the Moderns, etc. London, 1856, 8vo.
Keats, pp. 13, 14; reviewed by Leigh Hunt in *Fraser's Magazine* for December, 1859.

MAGAZINE ARTICLES.

Keats, John—Examiner, June 1, 1817, p. 345, July 6, 1817, pp. 428, 429, July 13, 1817, pp. 443, 444.—Blackwood's Edinburgh Magazine, vol. 3, 1818, pp. 519-524. — Blackwood's Edinburgh Magazine, vol. 7, 1820, p. 665 ; vol. 27, 1830, p. 633. — Indicator, by Leigh Hunt, vol. 1, 1820, pp. 337-352.—Quarterly Review, vol. 37, 1828, pp. 416-421.— Southern Literary Messenger, by H. T. Tuckerman, vol. 8, 1842, pp. 37-41.—Tait's Edinburgh Magazine, by T. De Quincey, vol. 13, N.S., 1846, pp. 249-254 ; same article, Eclectic Magazine, vol. 8, pp. 202-209. —Democratic Review, vol. 21, N.S., 1847, pp. 427-429.— United States Magazine, vol. 21, N.S., 1847, pp. 427-429 ; vol. 26, N.S., 1850, pp. 415-421.—Hogg's Weekly Instructor, with portrait, vol. 1, 1848, pp. 145-148 ; same article, Eclectic Magazine, vol. 14, pp. 409-415.—Chambers's Edinburgh Journal, vol. 10, N.S., 1848, pp. 376-380.—Sharpe's London Magazine, vol. 8, 1849, pp. 56-60.—Knickerbocker, vol. 55, 1860, pp. 392-397.—Temple Bar, vol. 38, 1873, pp. 501-512, —Edinburgh Review, July 1876, pp. 38-42.—Harper's New Monthly Magazine, vol. 40.

Keats, John.
1870, pp. 523-525 and vol. 55,
1877, by E. F. Madden, pp.
357-361, illustrated.—Scribner's
Monthly, by R. H. Stoddard,
vol. 15, 1877, pp. 203-213.—
American Bibliopolist, vol. 7,
p. 94, etc., and vol. 8, p. 94,
etc.—*La Revue Politique et
Littéraire*, by Léo Quesnel,
1877, pp. 61-65.—Argonaut, by
Reginald W. Corlass, vol. 2,
1875, pp. 172-178.—Canadian
Monthly, by Edgar Fawcett,
vol. 2, 1879, pp. 449-454.—
Century, by Edmund C. Stedman, illustrated, vol. 27, 1884,
pp. 599-602.

——*and his Critics.* Dial, vol. 1,
1881, pp. 265, 266.

——*and Joseph Severn.* Dublin
University Magazine, by E. S.
R., vol. 96, 1880, pp. 37-39.

——*and Lamb.* Southern Literary
Messenger, by H. T. Tuckerman, vol. 14, 1848, pp. 711-
715.

——*and Shelley.* To-Day, June
1883, pp. 188-206, etc.

——*and the Quarterly Review.*
Morning Chronicle, Oct. 3 and
8,1818 (two letters). Examiner,
11 Oct., 1818, pp. 648, 649.

——*an Esculapian Poet.* Asclepiad, with portrait on steel,
vol. 1, 1884, pp. 138-155.

——*Art of.* Our Corner, by J.
Robertson, vol. 4, 1884, pp. 40-
45, 72-76.

——*Cardinal Wiseman on.* Fraser's Magazine, by Leigh Hunt,
vol. 60, 1859, pp. 759, 760.

——*daintiest of Poets.* Victoria
Magazine, vol. 15, 1870, pp. 55-
67.

Keats, John.
——*Death of.* London Magazine,
vol. 3, 1821, pp. 426, 427.

—— ——*Verses on death of.*
London Magazine, vol. 3, 1821,
p. 526.

——*Did he really care for music?*
Manchester Quarterly, by John
Mortimer, vol 2, 1883, pp. 11-
17.

——*Endymion.* Quarterly Review,
by Gifford, vol. 19, 1818, pp.
204-208. — London Magazine,
vol. 1, 1820, pp. 380-389.

——*Forman's Edition of.* Macmillan's Magazine, vol. 49,
1884, pp. 330-341. — Times,
Aug. 7, 1884.

——*Fragment from.* Gentleman's
Magazine, by Grant Allen, vol.
244, 1879, pp. 676-686.

——*Genius of.* Christian Remem-
brancer, vol. 6, N.S., 1843, pp.
251-263.

——*Holman Hunt's "Isabel."*
Fortnightly Review, by B. Cra-
croft, vol. 3, 1868, pp. 648-657.

——*Hyperion.* American Whig
Review, vol. 14, 1851, pp. 311-
322.

——*Hyperionis, Libri* i-ii. Saturday Review, April 26, 1862, pp.
477, 478.

——*in Cloudland.* A poem of
thirty-one verses. St. James's
Magazine, by R. W. Buchanan,
vol. 7, 1863, pp. 470-475.

——*Lamia, Isabella, the Eve of
St. Agnes, and other poems.*
London Magazine, vol. 2, 1820,
pp. 315-321. — Indicator, by
Leigh Hunt, vol. 1, 1820, pp.
337-352.—Monthly Review, vol.
92, N.S., 1820, pp. 305-310.—
Eclectic Review, vol. 14 N.S.,
1820, 158-171.

Keats, John.

——*Leigh Hunt's Farewell Words to.* Indicator, September 20, 1820.

——*Letters to Fanny Brawne.* Athenæum, July 14, p. 50, July 21, pp. 80, 81, and July 28, 1877, pp. 114, 115.—Harper's New Monthly Magazine, vol. 57, 1878, p. 466. — Eclectic Magazine, vol. 27, N.S., 1878, pp. 495-498 (from the Academy). —Appleton's Journal, by R. H. Stoddard, vol. 4, N.S., 1878, pp. 379-382.

——*Life and Poems of.* Macmillan's Magazine, by D. Masson, vol. 3, 1860, pp. 1-16.

——*Marginalia made by Dante G. Rossetti in a copy of Keats' Poems.* Manchester Quarterly, by George Milner, vol. 2, 1883, pp. 1-10.

——*Milnes' Life of.* American Review, by C. A. Bristed, vol. 8, 1848, pp. 603-610.— Littell's Living Age, vol. 19, 1848, pp. 20 - 24. — United States Magazine, vol. 23, N.S., 1848, pp. 375-377.— Athenæum, Aug. 12, 1848, pp. 824-827. — Revue des Deux Mondes, by Philarète Chasles, Tom. 24, Série 5, 1848, pp. 584-607.—Eclectic Review, vol. 24, N.S., 1848, pp. 533-552.—Dublin Review, vol. 25, 1848, pp. 164-179. — British Quarterly Review, vol. 8, 1843, pp. 328-343.—Prospective Review, vol. 4, 1848, pp. 539-555.—Democratic Review, vol. 23, N.S., 1848, pp. 375-377. — Westminster Review, vol. 50, 1849, pp. 349-371.—Sharpe's London Magazine, vol. 8, 1849, pp. 56-

Keats, John.

60.—North British Review, vol. 10, 1848, pp. 69-96 ; same article, Eclectic Magazine, vol. 16, pp. 145-159.—New Monthly Magazine, vol. 84, 1848, pp. 105-115 ; same article, Eclectic Magazine, vol. 15, pp. 340-348. —Dublin University Magazine, vol. 33, 1849, pp. 28-35. —Democratic Review, vol, 26, N.S., 1850, pp. 415-421.

——*My Copy of.* Tinsley's Magazine, by Richard Dowling, vol. 25, 1879, pp. 427-436.

——*New Editions of.* Dial, by W. M. Payne, vol. 4, 1884, pp. 255, 256.

——*Le Paganisme poétique en Angleterre.* Revue des Deux Mondes, by Louis Étienne, Tom. 69, période 2, pp. 291-317.— Eclectic Review. vol. 8, 1817, pp. 267-275.

——*Poems of.* Examiner, by Leigh Hunt, June 1, July 6 and 13, 1817.—Edinburgh Review, by F. Jeffrey, vol. 34, 1820, pp. 203-213.—Tait's Edinburgh Magazine, vol. 8, N.S., 1841, pp. 650, 651.—Dublin University Magazine, vol. 21, 1843, pp. 690-703.—Edinburgh Review, vol. 90, 1849, pp. 424-430.—Massachusetts Quarterly Review, vol. 2, 1849, pp. 414-428.—Dublin University Magazine, vol. 83, 1874, pp. 699-706.—North American Review, vol. 124, 1877, pp. 500-501.

——*Poetry, Music, and Painting:* Coleridge and Keats. National Review, by W. J. Courthope, vol. 5, 1885, pp. 504-518.

Keats, John.

——*Recollections of.* Gentleman's Magazine, by Charles Cowden Clarke, vol. 12, N.S., 1874, pp. 177-204 ; same article, Littell's Living Age, vol. 121, pp. 174-188 ; Every Saturday, vol. 16, p. 262, etc., 669, etc.— Atlantic Monthly, by C. C. Clarke, vol. 7, 1861, pp. 86-100.

——*School House of,* at *Enfield.* St. James's Magazine Holiday Annual, 1875, by Charles Cowden Clarke.

Keats, John.

——*Thoughts on.* New Dominion Monthly (portrait), by Robert S. Weir, 1877, pp. 293-300.

——*Unpublished Notes on Milton.* Athenæum, Oct. 26, 1872, pp. 529, 530.

——*Unpublished Notes on Shakespeare.* Athenæum, Nov. 16, 1872, p. 634.

——*Vicissitudes* of *his fame.* Atlantic Monthly, by J. Severn, vol. 11, 1863, pp. 401-407 ; same article, Sharpe's London Magazine, vol. 34, N.S., 1869, pp. 246-249.

VII.—CHRONOLOGICAL LIST OF WORKS.

Price 6d.; Post Free, 7d.

No. I. READY SEPTEMBER 1st, 1887.

THE NATURALISTS' MONTHLY:

A JOURNAL FOR NATURE-LOVERS AND NATURE-THINKERS.

EDITED BY Dr. J. W. WILLIAMS, M.A.

The Naturalists' Monthly will contain—

1. Original and Recreative Papers on Popular Scientific subjects by well-known writers.
2. Articles on the Distribution of Animal and Plant Life in the British Islands.
3. Monographs on groups generally looked over by the Field-Naturalist, as the British Fresh-water Worms and Leeches in Zoology, and the Lichens and Mosses in Botany.
4. Accounts of Scientific Voyages and Expeditions.
5. Biographical Lives of the Greatest Scientific Men
6. "The Editor's Easy Chair"—a Monthly Chit-chat on the most important Scientific Questions of the day.
7. Reports of the Learned Societies.
8. General Notes and Correspondence.
9. Reviews of the latest Works and Papers.
10. Answer and Query Column for Workers.

The Naturalists' Monthly will be issued on the 1st of each Month. Annual Subscription, 7/- post free.

London : WALTER SCOTT, 24 Warwick Lane, Paternoster Row.

100TH THOUSAND.

CROWN 8vo, 440 PAGES, PRICE ONE SHILLING.

THE WORLD

OF CANT.

"*Daily Telegraph.*"—"Decidedly a book with a purpose."

"*Scotsman.*"—"A vigorous, clever, and almost ferocious exposure, in the form of a story, of the numerous shams and injustices."

"*Newcastle Weekly Chronicle.*"—"Trenchant in sarcasm, warm in commendation of high purpose. . . . A somewhat *remarkable book.*"

"*London Figaro.*"—"It cannot be said that the author is partial; clergymen and Nonconformist divines, Liberals and Conservatives, lawyers and tradesmen, all come under his lash. . . . The sketches are worth reading. Some of the characters are portrayed with considerable skill."

"May the Lord deliver us from all Cant: may the Lord, whatever else He do or forbear, teach us to look facts honestly in the face, and to beware (with a kind of shudder) of smearing them over with our despicable and damnable palaver into irrecognisability, and so falsifying the Lord's own Gospels to His unhappy blockheads of Children, all staggering down to Gehenna and the everlasting Swine's-trough, for want of Gospels.

"O Heaven! it is the most accursed sin of man: and done everywhere at present, on the streets and high places at noonday! Verily, seriously I say and pray as my chief orison, May the Lord deliver us from it."—*Letter from Carlyle to Emerson.*

London : WALTER SCOTT, 24 Warwick Lane, Paternoster Row.

CHEAP AND REVISED EDITION.
PRICE ONE SHILLING.

OUR
AMERICAN
BEING COUSINS:

PERSONAL IMPRESSIONS OF

THE PEOPLE AND INSTITUTIONS

OF THE UNITED STATES.

By W. E. ADAMS.

The author brings to his work acute penetration, a keen observation, a graphic picturesque style of presenting his impressions, and a quiet humour that finds expression in quoting amusing scraps from newspaper stories and sayings that aptly illustrate the case in point.—*New York Herald.*

That Mr. Adams is a person with a power for observing closely, describing impartially, and arriving at conclusions sustained by his process of argument, cannot be doubted by those who read his interesting work.—*New York Evening Telegram.*

We can heartily recommend Mr. Adams's book to those Englishmen who want to know something about America.—*Saturday Review,* 13th October 1883.

. . . We can say emphatically and truthfully of Mr. Adams's book that it is by far the best work of its kind we have yet seen. —*Knowledge.*

. . . Altogether, it is a sober, sensible book, by a level-headed observer of men and things.—*Pall Mall Gazette,* 12th November 1883.

People who want to know what Americans are like, and how they live, cannot do better than consult Mr. Adams's work, in which they will not find a single tedious page.—*Scotsman,* 13th September.

London : WALTER SCOTT, 24 Warwick Lane, Paternoster Row.

Crown 8vo, Paper Cover, Price Sixpence.

THE
TURKISH
BATH:

ITS HISTORY AND USES.

BY

FREDERIC C. COLEY, M.D.

CONTENTS :—The History of the Turkish Bath—How to take a Turkish Bath—Rules for the Turkish Bath—The Theory of the Turkish Bath.

London : WALTER SCOTT, 24 Warwick Lane, Paternoster Row.

Crown 8vo, Cloth,

PRICE ONE SHILLING.

ELOCUTION

BY

T. R. WALTON PEARSON, M.A.

Of St. Catharine's College, Cambridge,

AND

FREDERIC WILLIAM WAITHMAN,

*Lecturer on Elocution in the Leeds and
Bradford Institutes.*

London: WALTER SCOTT, 24 Warwick Lane, Paternoster Row.

www.ingramcontent.com/pod-product-compliance
Lightning Source LLC
Chambersburg PA
CBHW020112030726
47498CB00006B/2074